THE
YOUNG MERLIN
TRILOGY

THE
YOUNG
MERLIN
TRILOGY

PASSAGER, HOBBY,
and *MERLIN*

JANE YOLEN

Magic Carpet Books
Harcourt, Inc.
Orlando Austin New York
San Diego Toronto London

Requests for permission to make copies of any part of the work should be mailed
to the following address: Permissions Department, Harcourt, Inc.,
6277 Sea Harbor Drive, Orlando, Florida 32887-6777.

www.HarcourtBooks.com

Acknowledgments: Two of the novels included here are very loosely based upon
short stories, though each has been significantly expanded, developed, and
changed. *Passager* is based on "The Wild Child," and *Hobby* is based on
"Dream Reader," which are both drawn from the collection *Merlin's Booke.*

Passager and *Hobby* in their current form were originally published 1996,
and *Merlin* was originally published 1997, all by Harcourt, Inc.

First Magic Carpet Books edition 2004

Magic Carpet Books is a trademark of Harcourt, Inc., registered in
the United States of America and/or other jurisdictions.

Library of Congress Cataloging-in-Publication Data
The young Merlin trilogy/Jane Yolen.
p. cm.
"Magic Carpet Books."
Originally published in separate volumes
by Harcourt Brace in 1986, 1996, 1997 respectively.
Summary: Tells the story of the wizard Merlin from his abandonment at
the age of eight until, at twelve, he begins to understand the scope of his powers.
Contents: Passager—Hobby—Merlin.
1. Merlin (Legendary character)—Juvenile Fiction. [1. Merlin (Legendary
character)—Fiction. 2. Magicians—Fiction.] I. Yolen, Jane, *Passager,* 2004.
II. Yolen, Jane, *Hobby,* 2004. III. Yolen, Jane, *Merlin,* 2004. IV. Title.
PZ7.Y78Yo 2004
[Fic]—dc22 2004050409
ISBN 0-15-205211-9

Text set in Transitional 155
Designed by Lydia D'moch and Kaelin Chappell

ACEGHFDB

Printed in the United States of America

For Michael Stearns,
passager indeed

For Deborah and Robert Harris
and their boys

and

For Karen Weller-Watson,
who has her own magic

CONTENTS

PASSAGER

Passager:
A falcon caught in the wild
and trained by the falconer,
but not yet a mature bird.

Dark.

Night.

"He is still asleep, Mother."

"Three drops of the tincture will keep him still."

"Must we leave him?"

"We must."

"But he is so young."

"He is old enough. And we cannot keep him with us longer. There is danger to us all if he stays."

"But there is danger for him here."

"That is why we are leaving him high in the tree. The wild dogs cannot climb, nor fox nor wolves. In the daytime he will be quick and bright. He knows his nuts and berries, his mushrooms and ferns. You

have taught him well. He will be found soon enough by the wild men of the woods, the wode-wose, those without a place, whose villages have been erased by plague. They will hold him close as we cannot."

"But he is such a little bird, my child, my owlet, my hawkling."

"If you keep him longer, he will be your death. And ours. The church forbids it. God's law. And man's."

"I would die for him, Mother."

"Let him live for you. Come. Morning will be here soon enough and it is already time for Matins. We dare not miss more than that or there will be talk."

Light.

Day.

1. TERRITORY

THE BOY WAS SNIFFING AT THE ROOT OF A TREE, trying to decide if it was worth eating the mushrooms there, when he heard the first long baying of the pack. It was a sound that made the little hairs on the back of his neck stand up.

He turned at the sound and tried to find its source, but this was a dark part of the woods, and tangled. He was still considering when the first dog broke through the underbrush, almost at his heels.

It was a dun-colored dog, long-snouted, long-bodied. He had enough time to see that. He struck at it with the stick he always carried and it scrabbled away from him, whining.

He did not wait for the rest of the pack to find him, but jumped for the lower branch of the tree and scrambled up.

Finding its courage, the dun dog leaped for him and its teeth grazed his ankle, but it missed its hold.

The boy climbed higher, fear lending him quickness, strength. He was already high up in the tree when the rest of the pack found him. They broke through the brambles and bayed at the foot of the tree. There were seven of them, one more than the last time. The boy counted them off on his fingers—one hand's worth and a thumb had been the number the last time. There was a new one, a large yellow mastiff. He did not like the look of the dog. It was big and had brutal jaws. Clearly it had taken over leadership of the pack from the dun.

There was nothing the boy could do but wait them out. He had done it before. Patience was his one virtue, his necessity. Any business he had with mushrooms, grass, sky would wait. He settled into the crotch of the tree, making himself a part of it, as stolid, as solid, as silent as a tree limb, and waited.

After a while, the dun-colored dog wandered off, followed by two grey brachets. The mastiff growled at each desertion but could not hold them past their hunger. Not wanting to challenge them over the boy, now gone beyond their sight and therefore beyond their reckoning, the mastiff growled to the rest of the pack and walked off, stiff-legged.

They followed.

Only when another five long, silent minutes were gone did the boy relax. He whistled then, through dry lips. It was not a sound of relief or a boy's long, piercing come-here whistle, but sounded instead like one of the small finches. He had been many months in the woods, and what speech he still had was interspersed with this kind of birdsong. When frightened, he grunted the warning call of the wild boar. The dogs had surprised but not frightened him. In the forest he was too quick for them and they could not climb trees.

This was his patch of woodland. He knew every bush and tangle of it, had marked it the way a wolf does, on the jumbled overground roots of the largest trees. Oaks were his favorites, having solid and low climbing limbs, though he did not call them *oak*. He had his own name for them, a short bark of sound.

By damming up one of the little streams, he caught fish when he needed them, bright silvery things with spotted backs, scarcely a hand's span long. He ate them raw. He did not eat other meat, but rather spied on little animals for entertainment—baby rabbits and baby squirrels when he could find their hidey-holes, and badgers in their setts. They made him laugh.

At night he called down owls.

Once he had scared a mother fox off her kill by growling fiercely and rushing her, but found he could not eat the remains. When he returned to the kill the next morning, the meat was gone; the scent of fox lay heavy on the ground.

The first time he had been set upon by the wild dogs, he'd been forced off his own meager dinner. They had scattered his small cache of mushrooms and berries, mouthing each piece, then spitting them out again. When he came down from the tree, he found what he could of his food, but it all smelled bad; he choked when he tried to eat it. He went hungry that night.

It was not the first time.

He was very thin, with knobs for knees and elbows like arrowpoints, and scratches all over his body, which was brown everywhere from the sun. His thatch of straight, dark hair fell across his face, often obscuring his eyes, which were as green as the woodland, with gold highlights, like rays of sun showing through.

He had never made a fire, was even a little afraid to, for he believed fire was a younger son of the lightning that he thought the very devil, for it felled several of the great trees and left only glowing embers. Still, if he worshipped anything, it was the trees that sheltered him, fed him, cradled him.

He laughed at the antics of baby animals but could not tell a joke.

He imitated birdsong but could not sing.

He liked the way rain ran down his hair and across his cheeks, but he did not cry. An animal does not cry.

He was eight years old and alone.

2. HISTORY

THE WHOLE TIME HE HAD LIVED ALONE IN THE woods came to one easy winter, one very wet spring, one mild summer, and one brilliant fall.

A year.

But for an eight-year-old that is a good portion of a lifetime. He remembered all of that year. What he could not recall clearly was how he had come to the woods, how he had come to be alone. What he could recall made him uneasy. He remembered it mostly at night. And in dreams.

He remembered a large, smoky hearth and the smell of meat drippings. A hand slapped his—he remembered this, though he could not remember who had slapped him or why. That was not one of the bad dreams, though. He could clearly recall the taste of the meat before the slap, and it was good.

He also remembered sitting atop a great beast, so broad his legs stuck out on either side, and no beast in the forest, not even the deer, was that broad. He could still remember three or four hands holding him up on the beast, steadying him. Each hand had a gold band on the next-to-last finger. And that was a good dream, too. He liked what he could recall of the animal's musty smell.

There was a third dream that was good. Some sweet, clean-smelling face near his own. And a name whispered in his ear. But that dream was the haziest of the good dreams. The word in his ear was softer than any birdcall. It was as quiet as a green inchworm on the spring bough. So quiet he couldn't make it out at all.

The other dreams were bad.

There was the dream of two dragons, one red and one white, asleep in hollow stones. They woke and screamed when he looked at them.

That dream ended horribly in flames. He could hear the screams, now dragon and now something else, as if everything screaming was being consumed by fire. The smell he associated with this dream was not so different from the smell of the small hare he had found charred under the roots of a lightning-struck tree.

And there was another dream that frightened him. A dream of lying within a circle of great stones that danced around him faster and faster, until they made a blurry grey wall that held him in. Awake, he avoided all rocky outcroppings, preferring the forest paths. At night he slept in trees, not caves. The hollow of an oak seemed safer to him than the great, dark, hollow mouths that opened into the hills.

The scariest dream of all was of a man and a sword. He knew it was a man and a sword, though he had no name for either of them. Sometimes the man pointed the sword at him, sometimes he held it away. The sword's blade was like a silvery river in which he could read many wonderful and fearful things: dragons, knights riding great beasts, ladies lying in barges on an expanse of water, and—most awful of all—a beautiful woman with long, dark hair that twisted and squirmed like snakes, who beckoned to him with a mouth that was black and tongueless.

He could not stop the dreams from coming to him, but he had learned how to force himself awake before he was caught forever in the dream. In the dream he would push his hands together, cross his forefingers, and say his name. Then his eyes would open—his real eyes, not his dream eyes—and he would slowly swim up out of the dream and see the leaves of the trees outlined in the light of the moon or against the flickering ancient pattern of stars. Only, of course, once he was awake he could not remember his name.

So he named himself: Star Boy. Moon Boy. Boy of the Falling Leaves. Whatever it was on that day or night that caught his fancy. Rabbit Boy. Badger Boy. Hawk-in-stoop Boy. Boy. He never said these names aloud.

He did not think of himself in the intimate voice; did not think *I* am or *I* want or *I* will. It was always Star Boy is hungry or Moon Boy wants to sleep or Boy of the Falling Leaves drinks or

Rabbit, Badger, Hawk-in-stoop Boy goes up the hill and over the dale. Only these were said in images, not words.

Time for him was always *now* except in dreams. His history, all of the past, made no more sense to him than the dreams. And as more and more of his human words fell away—having no one to use them with—so did his need for past or future. His only memory was in dreams.

3. HAWK

IT WAS THE TAG END OF FALL, AND THE SQUIR-rels had been busy storing up acorn mast, hiding things in holes, burying and unburying. The boy had watched. He had even tried imitating them, but could never recall where he had buried any of the nuts, except for one handful, which when unearthed tasted musky and smelled of dirt.

A double V of late geese, noisy and aggravated, flew across the grey and lowering sky. He watched them for a long time, yearning for something. He did not know what. Shading his eyes with one dirty hand, he followed their progress until the last of them had disappeared behind a mountain.

"Hwonk," he cried after them. Then louder, "Hwahoooonk." He waited for a reply but none came. Unaccountably his right eye burned. He rubbed his fist in it and the fist was wet. Not a lot. But enough to make the dirt seem like filth.

Abruptly, he turned and ran down a deer track to the nearby river. He plunged in, paddling awkwardly near the edge, where the water pooled and slipped under exposed tree roots. He brought water up in cupped hands and splashed it on his face.

"Hwonk," he whispered to himself. Then he stood for a moment more. The cold water made his skin tingle pleasantly. When he climbed back up on the bank, the grass slippery underfoot, he shook himself all over like a dog and pushed the wet hair from his eyes.

He hummed as he walked, not a song, not even anything resembling a melody. It had no words, but a kind of comforting buzz. Then he yawned, his hand going up to his mouth as if it had a memory of its own. Finding a comfortable climbing tree, one he had used before, he got up in it, nestled in the place where two great limbs forked, and fell asleep. That it was day did not stop him from napping. He was alone. He made his own rules about time.

He had been asleep perhaps a quarter of an hour when a strange noise woke him; he did not move except to open his eyes. Caution had become a habit.

The sound that awakened him was not yippy like foxes or the long, howling fall of the dogs. It had teased into his dream and had changed the dream so abruptly that he awoke.

The call came closer.

Carefully he rose up a bit from the nest in the fork of the tree and crawled out along a thick branch that overlooked a clearing.

Suddenly something flapped over his head. He craned his neck and saw a hunting bird. She had a creamy breast and her tail had bands of alternating white and brown. Beak and talons flashed by him as she caught an updraft and landed near the top of a tall beech tree.

"Hwonk," he whispered, though he knew this was never such a bird.

No sooner had the falcon settled than the calling began again. It was an odd, unnatural, intrusive sound.

The boy looked down. On the edge of the wood stood a man, rather like the one in his dream, the one with the sword. He was large, with wide shoulders and red-brown hair that covered his face. There was a thin halo of hair around his head. When he walked across the meadow and then beneath the branch where the boy lay as still as leaves, the boy could see a round, pink area on the top of the man's head. It looked like a moon. A spotty, pink moon. The boy put his hand to his mouth so that he would not laugh out loud.

The man did not look up, did not notice the boy in the tree. His eyes were entirely on the tall beech tree and the magnificent bird near its crown. He swung a weighted string over his head and the string made an odd singing sound. The man whistled, and called, "Come, Lady. Come."

That was the sound that the boy had heard. The sound that had pulled him from his dream. Words.

The bird, though it watched the man carefully, did not move.

Neither did the boy.

4. CAPTURE

THE MAN AND THE BIRD EYED ONE ANOTHER FOR the rest of the short afternoon. In the tree, the boy watched them both. His patience with the scene below him was amazing, given that at one time or another his hands and his feet all fell asleep and he had an awful need to relieve himself.

Occasionally the bird would flutter her wings, as if testing them. Occasionally her head swiveled one way, then another. But she made no move to leave the beech.

The man seemed likewise content to stay. Except for making more circles around his head with the string, he remained almost motionless, though every now and again he made a clucking sound with his tongue. And he talked continuously to the bird, calling her names like "Hinny" and "Love," "Sweet Nell" and "Maid," in that same soft voice.

The boy took it all in, the bird in the tree, often still as a piece of stained glass, the sun lighting it from behind. And the man, with the thick leather glove on one hand, the whirring string in the other.

He wondered if the man would attempt, before night, to climb the tree after the bird, but he hoped that would not happen. The bird might then leave the tree; the tree, quite thin at the top, somewhat like the man, might break. The boy liked the look of the bird: her fierce, sharp independence, the way she stared at the man and then away. And the man's voice was comforting. It reminded the boy of something, something in his dreams. He could not remember what.

He hoped they would both stay. At least for a while.

When night came, they each slept where they were: the man right out in the clearing, his hands around his knees, the hawk high in her tree. The boy edged down from the tree, did his business, and was up the tree again so quietly none of the leaves slipped off into the autumn stillness.

He fell asleep once or twice that night but he did not dream.

In the morning the boy woke first, even before the bird, because he willed himself to. He watched as first the falcon shook herself into awareness, then the man below stretched and stood. If the boy had not seen them both sleeping, had only now wakened himself, he would have thought the two of them had not changed all the night.

The man was about to swing the lure above his head again when the falcon pumped her wings and took off from the tree at a small brown lark. The lark flew up and up, the hawk sticking closely behind, and soon they were on the very edge of sight.

The boy made slits of his eyes so he could watch, as first one bird and then the other took advantage of the currents of air. It almost seemed, he thought, as if the lark were sometimes chasing the hawk. He would have laughed aloud, but the man was too close beneath him.

The birds flew on, one above, one below, then circled suddenly and headed back toward the clearing, this time with the lark cleanly in the lead. The boy's hands in fists were hard against his chest as he watched, silently cheering first for the little bird, then for the following hawk.

Suddenly the lark swooped downward and the falcon hovered over it, a miracle of hesitation. Then with one long, perilous, vertical stoop, the hawk fell upon the lark, knocking it so hard the little bird tumbled over and over and over until it hit the ground not fifty feet from the man. Never looking away from her dying prey, the falcon followed it to earth. Then she sank her talons into the lark and looked about fiercely, as if daring anyone to take it from her.

The man walked quickly but without excess motion to the hawk. He nodded almost imperceptibly at her, speaking all the while in a continuous flow of soft words. Kneeling, he put one hand on her back and wings and with the other, the ungloved hand, hooded her so swiftly, the boy did not even see it till it was done. Then, stand-ing, the man placed the bird on his gloved wrist, gathered up dead lark and lure with his free hand, and walked smoothly toward the part of the forest he had come from.

Only when the man had disappeared into the underbrush did the boy unwind himself from the tree. Man, falcon, and dead lark were all so fas-cinating, he could not help himself. He had to see more. So he ran to the edge of the woods and, after no more than a moment's hesitation, rather like the hawk before beginning her stoop, he plunged in after them.

5. TRAIL

THE MAN'S PATH THROUGH THE TANGLE OF UN-
derbrush was well marked by broken boughs and
the deep impression of his boot heels. He was
not difficult to follow. That should have made the
boy suspicious, but he was too caught up in the
hunt.

In his eagerness to track the man, the boy ne-
glected to note anything about the place, though
this was a caution he had learned well over his
year in the wild. Still, he knew he could always
track back along the same wide swath. So perhaps
his hunter's mind was working.

The thorny berry bushes scratched his legs,

leaving a thin red map from hip to ankle, but he was used to such small wounds. Once he trod on a nettle. But he had done so before. It would sting for a while, then slowly recede, leaving only a dull ache that would disappear when his attention was on something else.

Nothing—*nothing*—could dampen his excitement. Not even the tiny prickle of fear that coursed wetly down his back, between his shoulder blades. If anything, the fear sharpened his excitement.

He walked a few feet, stopped, listened, though it was a blowy day, clouds scudding across a leaden sky. Mostly what he heard was wind in trees. He relied, therefore, on his eyes, and followed the man's passage through fern and bracken, and the prints alongside a fast-running stream.

Several hours passed like minutes, and still the boy remained eagerly on the man's trail. Only twice did he actually glimpse the man again. Once he saw the broad back, covered with its leathern coat.

Coat. That was a word suddenly returned to him. Right after, he thought, *jerkin.* He didn't know why the two words came together in his mind. So dissimilar and yet—somehow—peculiarly the same. He stopped for a moment, giving the man plenty of time to move on, out of hearing, then whispered the two words aloud.

"Coat." The word was short, sharp, like a wild dog's bark.

"Jerkin." He liked that word better and said it over and over again several more times. "Jerkin. Jerkin. Jerkin." The last time he said it loud enough to become instantly wary. But when he looked around there was no sign of the man, and he relaxed. Going down into the stream, he bent over to get a drink, lapping at it like an animal. But when he lifted his head out of the water, he smiled and said the two words again. "Coat," he said. "Jerkin."

He found the man's easy trail again and ran a bit, to make up for the lost time.

The second time he saw the man, the man had turned on the path and looked right at him. The boy froze, willing himself to disappear into the brush the way a new fawn and badgers and even red foxes could. He closed his eyes so that they would not shine, so that the blinking of his eyes would not reveal where he was.

It must have worked, because when he peeked through slotted eyes at the man, the man looked right at him and did not seem to see him at all, but kept on stroking the falcon's shoulder and whispering something to the bird the boy could not hear. The man cocked his head to one side as if considering, as if listening, but the boy remained absolutely still. Then the man turned away and walked on.

The boy followed, but more carefully now, stopping frequently to hide behind a tree or a bush or kneel down in the bracken or lie in the furze. He did not actually have to see the man to know where he was. They were on a well-worn trail now, a path packed down by many years of use. The boy could read the faint boot marks as well as a sharp impression of deer feet, the softer scrapings of badger, even the scratchings of grouse. A dog pack had left its scat, and recently, too. That made the boy nervous, and he remarked the tallest trees in case he had to climb quickly.

His slow reading of this worn pathway occupied

him, and he was not paying attention to what lay ahead. So he was surprised when the road turned and opened onto a man-made clearing. A farmhouse squatted near the center of it.

The farmhouse explained the new scents he had been ignoring. For a moment, he hesitated by the last trees and stared.

"House," he whispered, afraid and yet not afraid. "House."

6. DREAM

THERE WAS A TRAIL OF SMOKE FROM THE HOUSE chimney and for a long time the boy watched it dreamily. He could almost smell a joint of meat roasting. He could almost remember the crackle of the skin.

Then as the man neared the house a chorus of dogs began to howl. The boy remembered the yellow mastiff and its pack all too well. He stepped into the shadow of the trees and ran back down the road.

As soon as he was too far away to hear the dogs, he forgot them, for his stomach was growling. He had had nothing to eat all day.

It was growing dark, and foraging had to be a

quick and careful matter. He found a walnut tree and gathered nuts, as well as late-growth bramble berries. Then, picking up a rock to help him crack the nuts open, he chose a sleeping tree and scrambled up it for the night.

The nuts and berries were enough to stop the fiercest of the hunger pangs. When he fell asleep, the moon hanging over him orange and full, he began to dream.

At first he dreamed of food. Food cooking on a large, open hearth. Then he dreamed of dogs scrabbling on the hearthstones for their share of the cooked meat. The dogs were enormous, with eyes as great as saucers, as great as dinner plates, as great as platters. They stared at him and through him and—in his dream—his skin sloughed off. He watched, skinless, as the dogs ate his skin. Then they turned and stared at him with their big eyes and growled.

He woke in a sweat, shivering, and threw the nutshells down from the tree. He touched his arm and his leg to assure himself that he was whole, skin and all. Then he promised himself he would not fall asleep again.

But he did.

This time he dreamed of women in black robes and black wings who fluttered around him. They opened their mouths, and bird sounds came out.

"Cause!" they screamed at him. "Cause!"

He held out his hand in the dream and was surprised how heavy it seemed. When he looked at it, it was encased in a leather glove with thumb and fingers stiff as tree limbs.

Only one of the black-robed women alighted on his hand, her nails sharp as talons, piercing right through the glove.

The pain woke him, and his one hand hurt as if something had pierced the palm. He licked the hurt place and there was a thin, salty, blood taste.

This time he did not fall asleep again but waited, shivering, for the dawn to finally come with its comforting rondel of birdsong.

7. HOUSE

HIS USUAL MORNING INCLUDED A DRINK OF
water from the stream and a casual hunt for food.
But this morning he saw, through the bare liga-
ments of trees, the thin line of chimney smoke.

House. The word came unbidden into his mind.
And with the thought of house came the idea of
food. Not berries and mushrooms and nuts and
the occasional silver-finned, slippery fish torn
open and devoured bones and all, but *food.* He
was not sure what that meant anymore, but his
mouth remembered, and filled with water at the
thought.

So he crept back down the path to the edge of

the trees and squatted on his haunches, to stare avidly at the house.

There was a stillness about the house, except for that thread of smoke that seemed to unwind endlessly from the chimney.

At the prompting of his stomach, which ached as if it had suddenly discovered hunger for the first time, the boy left the sanctuary of the forest and ventured into the clearing. But he crept cautiously, like any wild thing.

There was a sudden flurry of sharp, excited cluckings. A familiar word burst into his head. *Hens!* He mouthed the word but did not say it aloud.

A high whinnying from one of the two outbuildings answered the hens. "Horse!" This time the boy spoke the word, his own voice reminding himself of the size of the beasts with their soft, broad backs that smelled of home.

He edged closer to the house, sniffing as he went, almost drinking in the odors, his chin raised and quivering.

Then the dogs began to bark and he turned sharply to run.

"Not so fast, youngling," said the man who loomed, suddenly, by his side and picked him off the ground by the shoulders. The man's voice was soft, not threatening, but the boy kicked and screamed a high, wild sound, and tried to slice at the man's face with his nails.

The man dropped him and grabbed both of the boy's hands with almost one motion, prisoning him as deftly as he had hooded the falcon.

The boy stopped screaming, stopped kicking, but he pulled away from the man, cowering, as if expecting a blow. His face was white, underneath the dirt, but his eyes were so dark as to be almost black, and hard and staring, the green-black of winterberries.

"Now hush ye, son," the man said in that soft, steady voice. "Hush, weanling, my young one, my wild one. Hush, you damned eelkin. I'll wash your face and hair and see what hides under that mop. Hush, my johnny, my jo." The soft murmuration continued as he marched the stone-faced boy all the way to the house and kicked open the door.

8. WILD THING

"MAG, FETCH ME A GREAT TOWEL. NELL, MY GIRL, put water in the tub. I've caught a wild thing that followed me home through the wood." The voice never got hard, though it got quite loud. "Quick now, the two of you. You know how it is with the wild ones."

Two women with kerchiefs binding their hair and long clay-colored gowns seemed to spring into being from the vast fireplace to do the man's bidding.

"Oh, sir," said the girl as she hauled the kettle full of water, "is it a bogle, all nekkid and brown like that? Is it a wodewose?" Her eyes grew big.

"It is a boy," said the man. "A sharp-eyed, underfed boy not much older than your own cousin Tom. And as for naked, well, he'd not been able to make clothes for himself after his own wore out, there in the middle of the New Forest, poor frightened thing. There are more than one of them put out in the woods nowadays. The nobles can send their extra sons off to a monastery as a gift of oblation, their hands wrapped in altar cloth and their inheritance clutched therein. But a poor man's son in these harsh times is oft left in the altar of the woods."

Mag appeared then with the toweling, shaking her head. "He looks not so much frightened, Master Robin, as fierce. Like one of your poor birds."

"Fierce indeed. And needing taming, I suspect, just like them. But first a bath, I think." The man smiled as he spoke, ever in that soft voice, while the two serving women clicked and clacked just like hens around the great tub. When at last they had emptied enough water in it and were satisfied with the temperature, Mag nodded and Master Robin dropped the boy in.

The boy had no fear of water, but it was not at all what he had expected. It was hot. *Hot!* River water, whatever the season, was always cold. Even in the lower pools—the ones he had dammed up for fishing—the water below the sun-warmed surface was cold enough to make his ankles ache if he stayed in too long.

He wanted to howl but he would not give his captors the satisfaction. He wanted to leap out of the bath, but the Robin-man's great hand was still on him. He didn't know what to do and indecision, in the end, made up his mind for him, for the fear and the warmth of the water together conspired to paralyze him. And the man kept speaking to him in that soft, steady, cozening voice.

The boy thought about the fawns in the forest, how they could disappear. How *he* had disappeared before when the man had stared at him. He closed his eyes to slits and willed himself to be gone, away from the man and his voice, away from the women and their hot water, away from the house.

But he had not slept well the last night, his dreams had prevented that. He was hungry, he was frightened, and he was—after all—only eight years old.

He closed his eyes and disappeared instead into a new dream.

In the new dream he was warm and safe and his stomach was full. He was cradled and rocked and sung sweet songs to by women in comforting black robes. They sang something he could remember just parts of:

> *Lullay, lullay, thou tiny child,*
> *Be sheltered from the wet and wild . . .*

But, he thought within the dream angrily, *I am wet and I am wild.* He made himself wake up by crossing his fingers, and found himself in a closed-in room.

Alone.

9. NAMES

UNTANGLING HIMSELF FROM THE COVERINGS, the boy crept to the floor and looked around cautiously. The room was low-ceilinged, heavily beamed. A grey stone hearth with a large fireplace was on the north wall. A pair of heavy iron tongs hung from an iron hook by the hearth. The fire that sat comfortably within the hearth had glowing red ember eyes that stared wickedly at him.

Suddenly something leaped from the red coals and landed, smoking, on the stones.

The boy jumped back onto the bed, amongst the tangle of covers, shaking.

The thing on the hearth exploded with a pop that split its smooth skin, like a newborn chick coming out of an egg. A sweet, tantalizing, familiar smell came from the thing. The boy watched as it grew cool, lost its live look. When nothing further happened, and even the red eyes of the fire seemed to sleep, he ran over, plucked up the hazelnut from the stones, and peeled it. His mouth remembered the hot, sweet, mealy taste even before he did.

He ran back to the bed and waited for something more to be flung out to him from the fire. Nothing more came.

But the nut had rekindled his hunger, and with it, his curiosity. He raised his head and sniffed. Besides the smell of roasted nut, beyond the heavy scent of the fire itself, was another, softer smell. The first part of it was like dry grass. He looked over the side of the bed and saw the rushes and verbena on the floor. That and the bed matting of heather supplied the grassy smell. But there was something more.

He scrambled across the wide bed and looked over the side. There, on a wooden tray, was food. Not mushrooms and berries, not nuts and silvery fish. But *food*. He bent over the food, as if guarding it, and looked around, his teeth bared.

He was alone.

He breathed in the smell of the warm loaf.

Bread, he thought. Then he spoke the name aloud.

"Bread!"

He remembered how he had loved it. Loved it covered with something. A pale slab next to the loaf had little smell.

Butter. That was it.

"But-ter." He said it aloud and loved the sound of it. "But-ter." He put his face close to the butter and stuck out his tongue, licking across the surface of the pale slab. Then he took the bread and ripped off a piece, dragged it across the butter, leaving a strange, deep gouge.

"Bread and but-ter," he said, and stuffed the whole thing in his mouth. The words were mangled, mashed in his full mouth, but he suddenly understood them with such a sharp insight that he was forced to shout them. The words—along with the pieces of buttered bread—spat from his mouth. He laughed and on his hands and knees picked up the pieces and stuffed them back in his mouth again.

Then he sat down, cross-legged by the tray, and

tore off more hunks of bread, smearing each piece with so much butter that soon his hands and elbows and even his bare stomach bore testimony to his greed.

At last he finished the bread and butter and licked the last crumbs from the tray and the floor around it.

There was a bowl of hot water the color of leaf mold on the tray as well. The bread had made him thirsty enough not to mind the color of the water and he bent over and lapped it up. He was surprised by the sweetness of the liquid and then knew—as suddenly as he had known the name of bread and butter—that it was not ordinary water. But he could not recall its name.

"Names," he whispered to himself, and named again all the things that had been given back to him, starting with the bread: "Bread. Butter. Horse. House. Hens. Jerkin. Coat." He liked the sound of these things and said the list of them again.

Then he added, but not aloud, *Master Robin, Mag, Nell*.

Patting his greasy stomach, he grunted happily.

He could not remember being this warm and this full for a long time. Maybe not ever.

Going back to the bed, he lay down on it, but he did not close his eyes. Instead he stared for a moment at the low-beamed ceiling where bunches of dried herbs hung on iron hooks. He had not noticed them before.

What else had he not noticed?

He sat up. There were two windows, and the light shining through them reminded him suddenly of the sun through the interlacing of the trees in the forest. This light fell to the floor in strange, dusty patterns. He crawled off the bed and over to the light, where he tried to catch the motes in his hand. Each time he snatched at the dusty beams, they disappeared, and when he opened his hand again, it was empty.

Standing, he looked out the window at the fields and at the forest beyond. There was a strong wind blowing. The trees were bending toward the east. He thrust his head forward, to smell the wind, and was surprised by the glass.

Hard air, he thought at first before his mind recalled the word *window.* He tried to push open the glass, but he could not move it, so he left that window and tried the other. He went back and forth between them, leaving little marks on the glass.

Angry then, he went to the wooden door in the wall next to the hearth and shoved his shoulder against it. It would not open.

So then he knew another name. *Cell.* He was in a cell. The fields he could see through the glass and the tall familiar trees beyond were lost to him. He put his head back and howled.

From the other side of the door came a loud, answering howl. One. Then another.

Dogs!

He ran back to the bed and hid under the covers and shivered with fear. There were no trees for him to climb. It was the first time in a long while that he had felt hopeless. That he had felt fear.

Wrapped in the covers, in the warmth, he fell asleep and did not dream.

10. THE BATED BOY

WHEN HE WOKE AGAIN THE ROOM WAS DARKER and the light through the windows shaded. There was a new loaf and a bowl of milk by the door.

The boy clutched the covers and listened, but he could hear no sound of dogs beyond the door. So he went over, warily, to the tray of food and cautiously looked at it sideways, through slotted eyes.

In a fit of sudden anger, an anger that smelled a good deal like fear, he kicked the bowl of milk over and screamed.

There was no answering scream beyond the door.

He went back to the bed, curled up in the

coverings as if he were in a nest, and willed himself back to sleep.

A few hours later he stood and urinated all
around the bed, marking it for his own. Then,
hungry, he went back to the door where the loaf
waited on the tray. He ate it savagely, stuffing
huge hunks into his mouth, and growling with
each bite. When he was done, he sniffed around
the place where the milk had spilled onto the
floor, but it had all soaked in.

Bored and angry, he paced back and forth between the darkened windows and the door, faster
and faster, until he broke into a trot. Finally he
ran around the room, until he was dizzy and out
of breath.

Then, standing in the very center of the room,
he threw back his head to howl once again, but
this time the howl died away into a series of short
gasps and moans. He went back to the bed and
curled into the covers and wept, something he
had not done in a year.

When the sounds of his weeping had stopped
and he drifted into a half sleep, the door into the
room opened slowly. Master Robin entered and
exchanged the empty tray for another, one with

trenchers full of meat stew and milky porridge. Then he went over and stared down at the boy in the bed.

"Who are you, boy?" he whispered. "And how come you to our wood?" Then he knelt down and sat on the bed, stroking the boy's matted hair and brushing it from the wide forehead.

At last he murmured in that soothing, low voice, "It does not matter. First we'll tame you, then we'll name you." He smiled. "And then you'll claim your own."

The voice, the words, the warmth entered into the boy's dreams and, dreaming still, he smiled and wiped his finger along his cheek. Then the finger found its way into his mouth and he slept that way until dawn.

The next day was a repeat of the first, and the next and the next. There were trays of food, by the bed or by the door. The hearth fire seemed always to be glowing with embers. Occasional hazelnuts popped mysteriously out onto the hearth. Milk and stew appeared as if by magic. But the boy did not see anyone else, though his sharp ears picked up sounds from beyond the door. Mag's voice singing. Or Nell's. And—occasionally—the whine of a dog.

By the fifth day, the room smelled and the floors bore the filthy reminders of the boy's woods habits. But this time when he woke, Master Robin was in the room waiting for him to wake. He brought the tray of food to the bed and the boy sat up, involuntarily licking his upper lip.

When Master Robin sat on the bed, the boy reached over to grab the loaf.

The man slapped his hand.

The sting did not hurt so much as the surprise. And then there was a sudden memory of that other slap, when he had been holding the joint of meat, back . . . back . . . before the woods.

"Forgive . . ." the boy croaked, as if trying out a new tongue.

The man hugged him fiercely, suddenly. "Nothing to forgive, young one. Just slow down. The bread will not run away. It is the manners of the house and not the manners of the woods you must use here."

The words meant less than the hug, of course. The boy sat back warily, waiting.

Master Robin broke the bread into two sections. Then he picked up a wooden stick with a rounded end and stuck it in the bowl of porridge. "Spoon," he said. "Do you remember any such?" He was silent for a moment, then held out the thing to the boy. "Spoon."

The boy whispered back, "Spoon." He put out his hand, and his fingers, closing around the handle, remembered. He ate the porridge greedily, but with a measure of care as well, frequently stopping to check the man's reactions.

"Good boy. So you are no stranger to spoons. How long were you in the woods then, I wonder? Long enough to go wild. Ah well, we will tame you. I am not a falconer for nought. I know how to man a bird, how to tame it. I have a long patience with wild things. Eat then. Eat and rest. This afternoon, after we cut your hair and dress you, I'll take you to the mews to see the hawks."

11. ROOM

THE MAN LEFT WITH THE TRAY, AND THE BOY did not even try to follow him. There had been a promise. That much he understood. A promise of a trip outside. It was enough.

However, he was too awake and too excited to nap, and wandered instead around the room; not restlessly this time, or angrily. Instead he went slowly, cataloging the room's contents. It was *his* room now. He had made it his first by marking it and then by feeling safe in it. Now he needed to know every corner of it.

There was the bed in the center, with its rumpled covers. The heather stuffing smelled a bit of mould now. But it was a comforting smell and he was used to it. The rush-strewn floor was likewise a bit off in its smell, like certain parts of the forest where there was too much bog and quaking earth. But the smell was familiar to him.

To one side of the bed was a small table that occasionally held a candle in an iron holder. He remembered its light when once he had awakened in the night. It had frightened him, then intrigued him. There was no candle now; instead a large bowl and jug stood there. He peered into them both. They were empty.

A great fire of logs burned on the hearth and to one side was a chair with a high back. It had arms carved with hawks' heads.

There was a tall wooden wardrobe standing by the side of the door. The handle for it was too high for him to reach. As if Master Robin's invitation had given him permission for exploration, he shoved the chair over to the wardrobe, scrambled up on it, and poked and pushed at the latch until he had gotten it undone. Of course he could not then open the door of the wardrobe because the chair barred the way. It took him another moment to figure this out. When he pushed the chair out of the way, the door swung open on its own.

Inside he found a pile of fur robes of dark, soft hides that smelled like the fox who had snarled at him, like the wolves whose scent he had been careful to stay upwind of. He ran his hand over the robes, first the smooth way, then the other, and laughed. There was nothing to fear here.

He tugged one of the robes from the closet and wrapped it over his shoulders. Going down on all fours, he threw his head back and howled.

There was an answering howl from the other room.

Dogs! He dropped the fur robe and raced back to the bed where he cowered under the covers.

After a while, the dogs were quiet and the boy crept back off the bed. He went to the window and looked out. A cow grazed on the open meadow, fastened by a chain to its spot. Near it two brown dogs ran back and forth frantically. He had never seen them before. The cow did not seem disturbed by them, but the boy moved away from the window so that they might not see him. Perhaps, he thought, they were new to the pack.

When he sneaked back, the dogs were playing still, this time running to fetch something. He saw it was a stick, which they brought over and laid at the feet of the man. It made the boy wonder that they were so tame. Perhaps, then, they were not of the pack after all.

Daringly, the boy put his hand to the window but the dogs never noticed. Nor did the man. With his forefinger, the boy drew a line down the middle of the window several inches long. | He looked at it and then, ever so carefully, drew a line across the middle. † After a moment's thought he drew a round thing on the top. ♀ Then he stopped and shook his head. The figure was incomplete. It needed something. He stood back from the window trying to puzzle it out, but the lines blurred together, faded.

When he turned around, Master Robin was standing in the room. Next to him were the two women. All three of them were smiling.

12. MEWS

THE OLDER WOMAN, MAG, STOPPED SMILING AS she crossed the threshold, wrinkling her nose as she glanced around the room.

The girl cried out, "Master Robin! The smell!"

"Hush ye!" the man said. He meant it sharply but his voice was not sharp.

The boy stood stone still as they approached him.

"Now, boy, now, little one . . ." the man's low, cozening voice began. He reached for the boy and, for a moment, that was all. Then his large hand gripped the boy's.

The boy trembled in the man's grasp. But when

the two women drew nearer and the girl put her hand on his arm, the boy snarled, a deep, chesty sound, and bared his teeth.

She drew back at once.

"You are a boy, not a beast," the man said gently. "You are a child of God, not . . ."

The boy's eyes rolled up in his head.

"Are you going to faint on me, boy?" the man asked.

But the boy was staring at the rooftree. "God," he whispered.

Mag and Nell crossed themselves quickly. The boy did the same, with his free arm.

"Nor Satan's imp then," Nell said.

"Of course not, you silly wench." For the first time there was exasperation in the man's voice. "Just a child. Gone feral. How often need I tell you so?"

Mag clucked like a hen and smoothed down her apron. "I am not so daft, Master Robin. Tell me what to do."

"The trews, woman. Bring them me."

She handed him the grey trousers with the drawstring waist. He prisoned the boy's two hands with his one big one, but not so as to hurt him, then with the other—and Mag's help—drew the pants on the boy one leg at a time.

At first the boy shook all over and whimpered. But he did not fight. He was too curious and, though he could not have explained why, found it vaguely familiar as well.

The shirt, when it went over his head, was more familiar still. He smoothed it down his chest, liking the feel of the cloth against him. In his memory there was another such shirt, one that came down to his knees, of a softer weave. It had kept him warm, he remembered, until it had—at last—fallen apart sometime in late spring. Only he did not remember spring. He thought of it as the warm time, when the river ran swiftly over the stones.

Then the man put a strange harness over the boy's head and around each shoulder and across his chest and back. It was plaited of rope and had a lead that Master Robin tied around his own wrist.

That reminded the boy of the cow tied out in the field, but he did not try to pull away. It made him feel as if he were part of the man and he liked that.

Master Robin sent the two women scuttling out of the room with a single word. "Go!" he said. They ran out like badgers scattering back to the sett. The boy laughed as they closed the door behind them. Master Robin laughed, too.

"So," the man said, "you can laugh and you can cry and you can speak some. You are no idiot left out by a father, no simpleton cast out of his town. I wonder why you were set adrift?" He stroked his beard as he spoke in that low voice.

The boy did not understand the question. What was *adrift*? What was *simpleton*? What was *town*?

"Would you like to see the birds in the mews?"

That at least he understood. *Birds.* He nodded.

"Well. And well." Master Robin pulled the boy close to him by the lead, then patted him on the head. "Tomorrow we will worry about your hair."

The birds were housed in a long, low building, with small windows of thinned-down horn.

"The mews," Master Robin said as they entered. He gave name to other things as they walked through the room. "Door. Perch. Bird. Lamp. Rafters."

Mimicking his tone, the boy repeated each word with a kind of greed, as if he could not get enough of the names. As he spoke, his face took on the same look it had when he had smelled the first loaf of bread, eyes squinting, head up, in feral anticipation.

They walked slowly, kicking up sawdust as they went. The boy took in everything as if it were both his first and his hundredth time in such a place.

He stood at last in front of a trio of hooded birds on individual stands where the heavy sacking screens hanging from the perches moved in the slight wind like castle banners. It looked as if he were about to speak. Instead he leaned forward, trembling, straining against the harness and lead.

Just then the two brown dogs, mixed-breed hounds, bounded into the mews.

The boy screamed and tried to run.

"Stay, damn you, stay!" the man shouted, whether to the dogs, the boy, or the hawks now agitated on their perches, their feathers ruffling —it was not clear.

The boy continued to shriek, his eyes wild.

The man turned to the dogs. "Sit!" he thundered, holding up his hand.

The two dogs immediately sat, tongues lolling. The smaller dog moved forward on its hind end, closer to the man, whining.

"Lie down," he thundered at them.

They lay down. The boy stopped shrieking but hid, trembling, behind the man. The hawks still fluttered, but at last even they quieted.

The man dragged the boy around in front of him by the rope. "These dogs will not harm you if I tell them so. They will guard you. They will be your friends."

The boy's trembling did not cease, but he was silent.

Holding the boy close, the man brought him to the dogs. "He is our boy," the man said. "You will *guard*. Now, *greet*." The larger of the two dogs crawled on its belly to the boy and licked his foot. The smaller dog followed. "Now, boy, pat their heads. Pull their ears. Let them hear thy voice."

He showed the boy what to do, but the boy was still too frightened, until the smaller dog suddenly rolled over on its back and showed the boy its belly. He touched its belly tentatively and then threw his head back and laughed. The dog flipped over and lay its quivering head on his bare foot. Bending down, the boy patted the dog's head. Then he pulled its ears.

"Dog," he said, in a voice that consciously mimicked the man's deep tones.

But he did not dare touch the larger dog. He just nodded at it.

"Enough for one lesson," the man said. "Time to eat." And they walked through the long, low building and into the slanting light of the fall day, which was a surprise to them both.

"Dog," the boy said as they walked past the corner of the building, where waist-high nettles hid the broken stones of an old wall. The small dog came to him, and trotted contentedly at his heels all the way into the house.

13 · DOG

THE SMALL DOG SLEPT AT THE BOY'S BEDFOOT until the middle of the night, when it got up and crept into the bed with him. The new heather in the mattress reminded the boy of the outdoors and the warmth of the dog recalled a time well before memory. He stirred slightly and slipped into a dream that was softer and gentler than any dreaming he had had in a year.

But after a while, the dog began to dream, too, of coursing after hare through the bracken. His legs scrabbled on the bedclothes and he scratched the boy's leg, not drawing blood, but pulling him swiftly out of sleep.

The boy woke disoriented and then, remembering, stuck his face in the dog's side, drinking deeply of the smell.

"Dog," he said, then raised his head and looked about.

The room was partly lit by light streaming in through the window. The boy rose from the bed, careful so as not to disturb the sleeping dog, and padded over to the lighted sill.

Under a full harvest moon, round and orange, shadows shifted across the field as if dream waves rolled across a dream ocean. The boy could just see the corner of the mews. And seeing the mews, he remembered the trio of birds on their perches shaking their wings in fear.

Something about those birds was important to him, but he did not know what. He only knew, suddenly and with fierce conviction, that he had to go to them.

He had gone to bed wearing the shirt Master Robin had put on him. It hung almost to his knees. He could not, himself, get into the trews. He did take the harness, though, thinking it part of his outfit, and carefully threaded his arms through it, wrapping the leadline around his arm three times to keep it out of his way. He began to tiptoe toward the door.

The dog roused at once, wagging its not inconsiderable tail.

"Dog," the boy whispered. The animal left the bed and came right over to him. "Sit!" But the boy's voice had none of the authority of the man's, and the dog remained standing at his side, its tail banging against his legs at every other beat.

The door was not open but it was not locked. The boy found this out when he pushed against it. It creaked only slightly. When he went out into the big hall, trailed by the dog, there was no one there but the mother dog drowsing on the hearthstones. Only coals remained of the roaring fire.

The boy was entirely silent as he moved across the floor, but the little dog's toenails clacketed on the stones. It was a comforting sound, though, and the boy smiled at it. The sound disturbed the older dog's sleep, however, and she looked up for a moment, lazily puzzled, before settling back with a contented sigh.

After several minutes the boy found the outside door. He had excellent night sight from his year in the forest, and besides, he could smell the outdoors through the space where door and wall did not exactly fit. It was a matter of moments till he could figure out the lifting of the latch, having watched the man do it.

He pulled the door open.

The little dog raced out before him, sniffing eagerly at the night air, then running to the nettles at the corner of the mews where it smelled the markings of its mother.

For a moment the boy stopped to look at the black-and-white shadow waves. There was a slight breeze blowing past the mews and over the field to the forest beyond. He could smell the musty mews, the birds, possibly the cow and horse in the stone barn beyond. Drawing himself up, recited the litany he had learned that afternoon: "Door," he said. "Perch. Bird. Lamp. Rafters." Then he walked to the mews door.

His hand was barely on the latch when a dog leaped upon him. Instinctively his hand went to guard his throat and the dog's teeth found only his wrist. In the moon's light he saw it was the dun dog and realized his mistake. The wind had been blowing *to* the woods. Not *from* it. He'd had no warning of the pack.

He screamed, a high piercing scream. The dun suddenly slackened its grip as the little brown dog, who'd slept so loyally on the boy's bed, leaped onto its back, savaging it with sharp teeth.

Then the pack was on them, the pair of grey brachets, the three small terriers harrying at the boy's heels. The yellow mastiff stood to one side, watching its packmates, waiting to move in at the kill.

And then just as suddenly the pack was scattered by a fierce, dark shadow. The loud, howling mother dog, having left the fire at the boy's first scream, waded into them. She found the terriers, grabbing one with her teeth and, shaking it three times fiercely, breaking its neck. The other two ran yipping across the meadow, disappearing entirely into the shadows of the corn.

The brachets wrenched about to face her and the dun threw the little dog off its back, and faced her as well. That could have been the end of her fight. There were still three against her. To save herself she needed to turn and run. But then, from behind her came a low, throaty growl. The yellow mastiff moved, stiff-legged, toward her, cutting off any retreat.

The boy began to tremble, but when the little dog hobbled to his side, favoring one front leg, and growled back at the mastiff, the boy's trembling became anger instead of fear. He unwrapped the leadline from his arm and in one savage movement flung himself on top of the dun dog, throttling its neck with the rope as hard as he could. He wasn't strong enough to kill it, but he managed to cut off its breathing and it dropped beneath him.

As if that were some kind of signal, the rest of the pack—the brachets and the mastiff—fell upon the mother dog. She screamed once, but the sound was drowned out by a sudden loud cracking of a horse whip.

"GET . . . AWAY . . . YOU . . . " came Master Robin's voice, and the whip snapped again, opening up the back of one of the brachets. And then again, the left front leg of the other.

The mastiff smelled the blood and would have stayed on, but the man banged its nose with the heavy leather butt end of the whip and it sprang away from the fight. Still growling, it backed up in its stiff-legged way till it felt the first of the corn at its back. Then it turned and melted away into the shadows. The brachets followed, howling. The dun, gasping, rose and stumbled after them.

Still trembling, the boy started toward the cornfield, but was caught up short by the man holding the trailing end of the leadline.

"Let them go," the man said, his voice soft again. "They will do us no harm now, my boy."

Suddenly the boy found himself sobbing. "Dog," he said. "Dog." He dropped to his knees and smothered the little dog with hugs.

Master Robin picked the boy up in one arm, the little dog in the other. "Our dogs will be well again," he said. "Let us tend them, shall we?"

"Yes," the boy said. "Yes." He buried his head against the man's broad shoulder for a moment, then looked past him. The mother dog, limping, bleeding slightly from a bite up high on her neck, was right behind. When he saw this, the boy relaxed and nuzzled against the man as a young pup will do with its own.

14. NAME

IT TOOK THEM THE REST OF THE NIGHT, MAN and boy working together, to bind up the dogs' wounds. The wounds were not deep, but there were many and they bled profusely. The mother dog lay patiently by the now-roaring fire while the man put poultices on the open sores and sewed up the raw edges of the bites with coarse black thread. But the smaller dog would not be still except with its head on the boy's lap.

By first light they were done, but with Mag and Nell stirring about, neither boy nor man wanted to try and sleep.

"The mews then?" the man asked at last.

"*Master Robin*—and after what happened?" Mag protested, waving her hands about.

The boy gave her a pitying look.

"The birds still must be tended," the man said. "And I will take the whip. But I doubt that pack will be back. There's easier pickings in the woods."

They went out, man and boy, together.

Except for patches of blood-sodden earth and the dead terrier by the mews door, there was no sign of the war that had been fought. They buried the terrier—so small and pathetic in the morning light. The boy did not wonder at it. He had seen his fill of dead things in the wood.

The mews was cool and shadowy; it smelled of must and age. The boy went eagerly in after the man, and in a quiet voice recited his lesson.

"Door. Perch. Bird. Lamp. Rafters."

The man turned to look at him and nodded, careful not to laugh. They stared at one another for a long moment, then tracked through the sawdust on the floor side by side.

When at last they were before the trio of birds, Master Robin stood, hands behind his back, nodding. The boy echoed his stance.

"Bird," the boy said, his voice husky.

"Mine," the man said as if in answer. He took care to speak as solemnly as the boy. "Mine because they have given some part of themselves to me. But not all. And not forever." He let the boy take that in before continuing. "I would not want them to give me all. And every day I must earn their trust again."

"Again," the boy said, nodding.

"With wild things," the man said, turning his head slightly to watch the boy, his eyes narrowing, "there is no such word as *forever*."

The boy listened intently.

"I stood three nights running with the goshawk there," said the man, nodding toward the bird furthest to the left. "He was on my fist the whole time."

"Tied?" the boy asked. It was a new word and an old one for him.

"Aye."

The boy seemed to consider this, as if he knew it had been a wise thing to do. "Tied."

"When he bated, I put him back on my fist again. And again. And again. I sang to him. I spoke words to him."

"My hinny, my jo," the boy said in a passable imitation of the man's voice. The man was momentarily stunned. "My hinny, my jo," the boy repeated.

"Aye. And stroked his talons with a feather and gave him meat. And, after three days without sleep, he allowed himself to nap on my fist. He *gave* himself to me in his sleep."

"In his sleep," the boy said, wondering if the hawk could dream.

"The peregrine there," Master Robin said, indicating the middle bird. "Now she is my oldest bird. A beauty. An *eyas*. Like all females, she is strong and calm."

"Eyas. Oldest." The words were equally strange to the boy.

The third bird suddenly stirred.

"That means I took her from the nest myself. Nearly lost an eye doing it, but ..." The man stopped, aware the boy was no longer listening. Instead he was straining to watch the third bird, staring up at it.

"Ah, that one. He's a *passager*, wild caught but not yet mature."

The hawk stirred again, as if it knew it was

being talked about. The bell on its jess rang out.

At the sound, the boy jumped back.

"You like my merlin best, then?" the man asked in his low voice.

The boy turned sharply, stared at the man wide-eyed. His mouth dropped open and he put his hands out as if he had suddenly been turned blind.

Master Robin gathered the boy in his arms. "What is it, then? What is it, my boy, my passager, my wild one? What did I say? What have I done?"

The boy tore from his arms, and turned again to the bird who, unaccountably, began to rock back and forth from one foot to another, its bell jangling madly.

As if he, too, were a bird on a perch, the boy began to rock back and forth. "Name," he cried out. "Name."

The man stared at the boy and bird and finally, with a shock of understanding, he plunged his hand into the nearby water barrel. Then he reached for the boy. With his finger he drew a cross on the boy's forehead, one swift line down, a second across, under the tangle of elfknots in his hair.

"I baptize thee Merlin, my child. Somehow your name is the bird's. In the name of the Father and of the Son and of the Holy Spirit. Amen."

"Amen," the boy said, and smiled up at the man. "I . . . am . . . Merlin." And memory as well as language came flooding through him as he was given back his own true name.

Light.

Morn.

"Mother, I think often of my lost one, my hawk-let, my Merlin."

"Do not say his name here, my daughter. Do not summon up the past."

"But, Mother, he is not just past, but future as well. As are all children."

"You must think upon the Lord God, my daughter."

"Will He think upon my child?"

"God watches over all wild things, my daughter, for they neither worry about nor pity their own con-

dition. Perhaps your son is the greater for this exile in the woods."

"Perhaps, Mother, he is dead."

"Then he is with God the sooner. And we are still here, laboring away at our daily rounds. To your prayers now. Think no more of what has been, but what shall be."

The bells ring for matins, like the sound of a tamed hawk's jesses, like the voices of angels making the long and perilous passage between heaven and earth.

HOBBY

Hobby:
A small Old World falcon
or hawk that has been trained
and flown at small birds.

Dark.

Night.

The boy dreams of a bird, its breast as red as flames, rising to heaven singing, and wakes to smoke.

Fire licks the edges of the thatched rooftop, bright shooting stars let loose from a chink in the chimney. The house is suddenly aglow.

A dog howls.

Then a second.

Bells from the mews jangle frantically.

The scream of a woman tears the air. "Master Robin. Master—" Her voice is cut off.

A door bursts open and a figure appears. It is a boy carrying the body of a dog. They are haloed by fire. Gently, he places the dog on the ground, well away from the flames, then turns to go back in.

Someone else stumbles through the door. A woman, by the clothes. But she has no hair, it having been consumed by the fire. The boy catches her before she falls. He lays her down by the dog's side, turns.

The roof falls in with a great whoooosh of sound. No one else alive can come out of that house. No one alive can go in.

Sparks fly to the mews, to the barn and, like the house, they are devoured whole.

After a long while—a day, a lifetime—the flames are silent.

Birds sing from the nearby woods.

Light.

Day.

1. LIES

THE BOY BURIED THEM ALL IN A SINGLE GRAVE: dog, woman, and the charred remains of the others. Of the birds in the mews there was nothing left to bury. Nothing except one tiny brass bell from the littlest hawk's jesses. He pocketed this treasure without thinking.

A single grave. Digging five separate ones would have been too hard for him. At twelve he did not yet have his full strength. But he did it also because he could not bear that they should be apart: Master Robin, Mag, Nell, the two dogs. They were his family, all that he had had for the past four years. A family, he knew, must stay as one. He did not know how he knew it, but he did.

He would have thrown himself into the pit as well, as penance for not understanding his dream of the bird in flames and rising sooner. The guilt of all their deaths, of the fact that he was still alive, was almost too great to bear. But there was something in him, a kind of sense as strong as that of sight and hearing and smell, that told him to stay alive.

"And remember," he whispered to himself. By that he meant *remember* Master Robin, who had rescued him from the woods and taught him to read, both the words on a slate and the passage of a hawk across the sky. And remember Mag, who had kept him cosseted and fed. And Nell, who had taught him all the games he had missed as a child. And the dogs who guarded him at night and brought back thrown sticks and licked his face. And the falcons who came to his hand. If he remembered them, they would still be alive, in some odd way. Not alive *beside* him, but *inside* him.

He said a prayer over the grave, a prayer that took in the fact that though his own world seemed to have ended, the world seemed still to go on. And he spoke words he vaguely recalled in Latin, though he didn't know it was Latin he was recalling. *"In nomine Patris,"* he said.

And he told himself the first of many lies he would tell that fall. "I will not cry."

It was a lie before he left the farmsteadings.

He drove the old dry cow before him, led the great-footed mare. They had been out in the pasture and thus been spared of the fire. He wore his nightshirt tucked into a pair of singed trousers and carried the one pair of boots the fire had not taken, their lacings tied together and slung across his back. They were not his boots; his boots were ash. These were an old pair of Master Robin's boots that had been set out by the door, too dirty for Mag's fresh flooring. He would grow into them in time.

He had slaughtered the two hens, after gathering their last two eggs, because he couldn't herd them properly and didn't want to leave them for the foxes. And he cooked them on the embers of the house and mews to have food for the long walk ahead. One chicken and the eggs he finished before leaving, for grave digging was hard work and he was famished. The other chicken he put in the leather pouch, along with the little bell.

He did not know where he was going, exactly, but he could not bear to stay at the ruin of the farm. Once he had gone to a great fair with Master Robin and it had been several days' walk west. If he could find it again, he thought he might sell both cow and horse there and make a new life on his own.

Chewing thoughtfully on a drumstick, the boy turned to look one last time at the burned-out hulk that had been his home for four years. *That* was when he began to cry, the tears falling quickly.

But he did not make a sound as he cried. He was afraid if he started, his howling would never stop.

The woods were cold and spattered with sunlight wherever the interlacings of yellowing leaves thinned out. For a while he rode the horse, a big-hearted Dales mare named Goodie. She had a walk better suited to the plow and he had to ride her bareback. Still, he was such a light weight, she hardly noticed him.

The cow plodded placidly behind the horse. They made an uncommon pair, but so long together in the same barn and pasture, they were as easy with one another as old gossips. The boy napped twice on the horse's back. Each small sleep brought him the same snippet of dream: the flame-breasted bird singing of danger. He forced himself to wake and mourned his lost family at each waking.

By nightfall, not only the leaves had thinned out, but the trees as well. The boy got off the horse, leading both horse and cow behind by their halter ropes. He did not want to chance that either might run off, startled by some new sight or sound.

The broad and knotted holm oaks gave way to a large meadow. Still in the oak shadow, the boy listened intently to a stirring of nearby grasses.

Suddenly a herd of deer, small and brown and dappled with moonlight, passed by so close to him, he could see their liquid eyes. Goodie whinnied and, at that, the deer were gone, as if by magic.

Magic! For a moment the boy wondered if the deer were a sign. But though he was used to dreams, both waking and sleeping, he had never dreamed of deer. He let out a deep breath, which surprised him, for he had not known he was holding it.

"Now, Goodie," he said to the horse. "Now, Churn," to the cow. "We must rest the night. I promise you will be safe."

He tied them loosely to a low tree branch, then settled himself up in the crotch of one of the oaks.

"I am too tired to dream," he called down to them, hoping that by saying the words aloud they would become true. He was afraid to dream again of the fire bird, afraid to be reminded once more how his refusal to wake in time, his inability to understand the dream in time, had robbed him of his family. "I will not let myself dream," he called to the horse and cow.

Another lie.

2. WALLS

HE DREAMED OF HOME. NOT THE HOME HE HAD last seen, burned and blackened, but a different home. This one was stone upon stone, several towers high, with tile roofs and stone walkways. Only women lived there, dressed like crows. They pecked at him with tiny, quick beaks. They beat at him with black wings. Then, at a high-pitched whistle, they left off abusing him and rose into the air, circling the towers and then down to a courtyard where a priest dressed in black called them down like a falconer.

The boy woke, shivering, and for a moment was eight years old again, alone and in the forest. "Horse," he reminded himself, staring down into the darkness. "Cow." They had been among his first words when Master Robin rescued him. Then he mumbled his own name and, with that, fell asleep once again to dream—as boys often do—of dragons.

When he woke for good, it was dawn. Birdsong assaulted him. From the tree he could look far across the meadow to a sudden blue lake, winking in the light, like a signal lantern. To the right of the lake was a swath of sandy shingle. To the left was something very like a high wall.

"A wall," he said aloud. "A wall means people." It had to be a town's gate. The town he and Master Robin had visited. He smiled and, still sitting in the tree, fetched out the last pieces of chicken from his leather pouch. There was no need to keep them any longer, for there would be food aplenty in the town. He ate contentedly.

When he was done, he rubbed his sleeve across his greasy mouth. He thought that Mag would have clapped him hard on the ear for so doing. She had cloths at the table for such. How often had she told him: "Easier to wash them, than to wash thy shirt, boy."

But he had no table cloths. And no wash water.

And no Mag either. The thought threatened to unman him once again and, in order not to cry, he leaped down from the tree. He hit the ground solidly, frightening the cow but not the stolid Goodie, who only shook her head in annoyance.

If he wished for a cloth, he wished even more for some drinking water, for the chicken had awakened a sudden thirst in him. But his skin bag was empty. Still, ahead lay the lake and the wall, the one meaning water and the other company. He got up on Goodie's back and, holding Churn's long halter rope, pulled her after them, though she clearly wanted to browse the meadow.

No amount of kicking with his bare heels moved Goodie out of her walk, and so the boy relaxed and watched as swallows crisscrossed before them, chasing after insects the horse and cow kicked up.

It took them the greater part of an hour to get close enough to see that the wall was not part of a town but marked the site of a large ruin. They picked their way carefully through the debris of some old outworks, the broken weedy remains of a road. Goodie stepped high over the crumbled stones. The boy had to yank several times hard on the cow's rope to encourage her to follow. But when at last there was a wind off the lake and she smelled the water, Churn picked up her legs in a fast trot, suddenly almost young again.

At the lake's edge, the two animals drank eagerly. But after a handful of water, the boy went over to the ruins, curiosity getting the better of thirst.

There was a series of high walls, all broken at the top, though several half-roofs of dark tile still guarded the upper rooms from weather. At his approach, a dozen doves clattered up into the light, proving that the place was long deserted.

The ruins reminded him, oddly enough, of his dream: the same high walls, the half-gabled roofs. They lacked only the crow women in their black robes, and the priest. He wondered what people had lived in this place and for a moment closed his eyes, as if that could help him envision them. But he could not imagine anyone here. It was too long empty. Too musty. Too cold.

He stepped over some broken stones and found himself in a kind of courtyard, clearly once a garden, for there were several ancient fruit trees bent like old men, the browned remains of unharvested fruit by the twisted roots. Stones lined out a series of still-neat borders but nettles had taken over the plots of earth. In the very center of the garden was a mosaic, partially covered with dirt and uneven where the ground had shifted beneath it. The boy could make out some sort of spade-bearded, fish-tailed god; it looked a lot like Master Robin, broad shouldered and with red-brown hair. The boy turned away quickly before he had time to weep, his hand going to the leather pocket where the hawk's bell rested.

It was when he stepped through two massive upright pillars, grooved by human hand and pitted by wind and storms, that he smelled something that was neither meadow, nor lake, nor the musty, stale scent of the ruins.

It was smoke.

3. SMOKE

HE KNEW THAT SMELL. NOT THE ODOR OF A house burning down, still so fresh and bitter to him. It was the smell of a cookfire, with meat on a spit.

This time, though, caution claimed him. He crept to the side of the garden wall and, using it to shield his back, inched up a set of stone steps that were still preserved and whole.

At the top the stairs broke off awkwardly, but the boy could look down over the entire ruins. He saw the cookfire. It was in one of a series of out-lying half-roofed houses beyond the main walls. A man dressed all in black was poking at the fire with a stick. He reminded the boy of the priest in his dream.

The boy almost called out then, but there was something about the man's shoulders he did not care for, a tense roundness, like a hawk right before it mantled, throwing one wing out, then another, to protect its food. Those shoulders belonged to a greedy, angry man, the boy thought. He needed to find people, but—even more—he needed to be careful.

Taking his bearings, the boy ran back down the stairs, turned in through a massive archway, and threaded his way as quietly as possible through the remains of the halls, now only broken masonry and vines.

When he found the cookfire, more by smell than by the mapping in his head, creeping up to peer through the doorway, the man was gone. A rabbit roasting on a spit was not quite done.

He heard a low growl behind him and slowly turned.

In the ruined hallway, glaring at him, was a massive dark dog, its teeth bared.

The boy backed up a step, toward the spit, and moving very slowly, took the boots from around his neck. They were the closest thing to a weapon he had. He was about to fling them at the dog when a whistle shrilled through the air and the dog's ears raised.

"Hold, Ranger!" came a coarse, raw-edged voice from beyond the doorway, and the dog's legs tensed, though it did not otherwise move.

The man stepped into view with hair the grey of old bowstring and a sparse, tired mustache. One eye was half shuttered by scarring. He wiped his nose with his black sleeve but never took his eye off the boy. "Watch!" he commanded the dog.

"Sir . . ." the boy began, knowing full well the man was no kind of gentry by his voice and clothes. Still, he did not want to provoke the man; he had no idea how dangerous the man was. "Sir, help me. I have been burned out of my house. My family died in the fire. And I am . . ."

"I think you are a thief, boy. Those boots you hold are much too big for you. That horse and cow too rich for such as you. I think you should be taken to the local sheriff and . . ."

"I think you are, yourself, a thief and shall not take me there," the boy answered hotly.

The man laughed briefly and horribly, then took two large steps forward so that the boy could smell his terrible breath. He grabbed the boy's shoulder. "Thief I may sometimes be," he said, his raw voice still full of the laugh, "but I will not be called so by a mere boy." In one swift move, he ripped the boots from the boy's hands and threw him down, kicking him in the side almost as an afterthought. It was not hard enough to break any bones, only hard enough to show who was master.

"Ranger," the man said, "keep!"

The dog stood over the boy, growling in a quiet monotone.

"Ranger will not hurt you, boy," the man said with a chuckle. "Lest, of course, you move." He bent over and tore the leather pocket from the boy's side. Opening it, he found only the charred bell, greasy from chicken, and threw it on the ground in disgust.

The boy bit his lip to keep from crying out; the loss of the little hawk's bell hurt more than the kick had.

Sitting down at the fire, the man took off his own boots, which were scarcely more than two pieces of leather tied onto the foot. Slipping on Master Robin's boots, he sighed. "Just my size," he said, and laughed again. "Or close enough that makes no difference. One's not a man without proper boots, don't you think?" He stretched his long legs closer to the fire and sniffed the air appreciatively. "Rabbit's about done, boy. If you lie quiet, I might just give you a piece."

"I want none of you," the boy said. "Or your rabbit." His bravado was encouraged by the fact that his own belly was full enough with chicken. But when he spoke, the dog growled again and moved, if possible, even closer to him, its breath as bad as its master's.

"Not now, perhaps," the man said. "But anon." He began to eat greedily, smacking his lips as he did so. His manners, the boy thought, would have earned him a great clap on the head from Mag.

The boy lay still, ribs aching, and fell into a kind of reverie. In it he saw the man felled by a thrown stone, crumpling to the ground, where he lay haloed in blood. A dog licked the blood till it was gone, then put its reddened muzzle into the air and howled. But when the boy woke, the man was very much alive and the dog had not moved from its guard position. Then the boy knew that it had just been a dream. His eyes began to tear up and he willed himself not to cry.

4. FOR SALE

THEY STAYED IN THE RUINS FOR THE REST OF that day and night. Much of the time the boy was bound, loosely when the dog was nearby, tightly when it was gone hunting with the man. No amount of twisting and rubbing the rope against stone seemed to help.

The boy fell to dreaming more and more, and his dreams were of blood and fire, fire and blood. They exhausted him. They confused him. He wondered if they had any meaning beyond disturbing his sleep.

At dawn the man seemed to make up his mind about something. "Not coming then," he mused aloud. "Well, it was worth the try."

"What was?" the boy asked, thinking the man was speaking to him, and receiving a cuff on the ear for asking. It was hard enough to make him fall over, hard enough to set his ear ringing, like the bells of a captive hawk.

The man picked him up, setting him against a fallen pillar. "Now, boy, don't ask me questions. I do not like it. Give me answers. That will sweeten my hand."

The boy nodded, not chancing another blow.

"What is your name then, little thief?"

The boy thought for a moment. His name was Merlin, like the hawk in Master Robin's mews. But that was his name with the family. And the family was no more, buried under earth and gone to worms. Names could have power, he knew that instinctively. His own name had given him back his power of speech, had given him a past. And even though this man's power was great, it was a black, evil thing. He would give the man no more power than he already had.

"Hawk," the boy said. "My name is Hawk." It was close enough.

The man laughed. "A lie of course. You hesitated too long for the truth. And who would have named such a small, darkling boy such a strong, powerful name? But no matter. I will call you Hawk. It is conveniently short. And as for me, you can call me . . . Fowler . . . for I have mastered you as a falconer does a bird."

The boy almost spoke back then, for if he knew anything well from his years with Master Robin it was falconry. This man was no fowler. And he was no master either. But the boy bit his lip and said nothing.

"We are but a day out of Gwethern, a busy little market town, where I will sell your labor to a farmer and collect the wages. And you will not run, little bird, else I will have the sheriff on you. As will the farmer." He smiled. It did not improve his looks. "Do you understand me?"

The boy glared.

Fowler raised his hand for a slap.

"Yes," Hawk said, begrudging the syllable.

"Yes what?"

"Yes . . . sir." The second syllable was even more grudging.

"I will unbind you, hawkling," Fowler said. "But my dog will be your leading strings. Mind him, now. He has a foul temper. Fowler and Fouler."

He laughed at his own joke, the sound coming out jerkily.

Hawk did not smile. He stood slowly and held out his hands. Fowler undid the ropes on the boy's wrists.

"Watch!" he said to the dog, and Ranger took up a position at Hawk's heels. He did not leave that place for the rest of the long day.

They walked for a while before Fowler mounted Goodie. The big horse trembled under his weight, not because the man was heavy but because he was unfamiliar and kept at her with his rough boot heels.

They made a strange company, but not so unusual for a market town road: a half-grown boy, nervously in front of a menace of a dog; a massive, black-clad man on a plowhorse, leading an old cow by a rope.

No one will wonder about us, Hawk realized. *No one will question the man's right to sell us all: horse, cow, boy. Even dog.*

Just as he came to that awful conclusion, a large tan hare started across the road.

"Ranger, stay!" Fowler called out, though the dog had made no move toward the hare. But Fowler should have paid more mind to the horse. Unused to the road, upset with the man on her back, startled by the hare, the normally placid Goodie suddenly shied. She took one quick step to the left and then rose up onto her back legs.

Fowler was flung off, landing with a horrifying *thud!* His head whacked against a marker stone and, as he lay there, unmoving, blood flowed out of his nose, staining his mustache.

The dog left the boy's heels and went over to its master. It sniffed the man's head uncertainly, then sat down, threw back its head, and howled.

For a moment Hawk did not know what to do. He was stunned by the scene, which was—and was not—the very dream he had had: stone, blood, howl. He remembered, bleakly, the other dreams he had had that had come true. The dream of the flame-breasted bird. The dream of the whistling black-coated man. And now, most horribly specific, this.

He did not know if his dreams were wishes so powerful they came true, though he had certainly never wanted the fire that had destroyed his life. He did not know if he had the ability to see slant-wise into the future. Either—or both. He did not know and was afraid to know.

The dog kept on howling, an eerie sound, awful and final.

And tears, unwanted, uncalled-for, fell from Hawk's eyes. He could not seem to stop crying.

5. THE TOWN

"WHY?" HAWK ASKED ALOUD. BY THAT HE MEANT: Why was he crying at the death of the awful Fowler, a man who had beaten him and tied him up and would have sold him? Why was he crying now when he had not cried—not really—at the death of those he loved? Master Robin, Mag, Nell, the dogs, the hawks. "Why?"

Still crying, he got up onto Goodie's back, for she was once again the stolid plowhorse, and they started down the road, with Churn right after.

Hawk wiped his nose on the back of his sleeve, thinking that he had not been able to touch the man nor bring himself to bury him. He only wanted to be gone away, from the man, the stone, the blood, the howls. He was almost a mile along before he could no longer hear the dog.

Without wanting to, Hawk fell into a reverie on Goodie's back and began to daydream. It was a very odd dream this time—of a wizard and a green castle. There was a bird in the dream as well, eating an apple, then spitting out a green worm. When the worm touched the ground, it grew to dragon size, then took to the air, its great wings whipping up a wind. Hawk woke sweating, though the day was cool. Was it another dream of the future? And what future, he wondered, could include all those things?

As suddenly as the dream ended, so did the path. It opened instead onto a real road that was rutted with use. For the first time there were other travelers: farmers with carts piled high with vegetables—carrots and neeps and green onions. Whole families in wagons, the children packed in with the caged fowl. Here and there single riders trotted on fine horses, not plowmares like Goodie. Hawk felt entirely awkward and dirty, ragged and alone. But at least he saw nothing like a wizard, a castle, an apple, or a worm.

He was hungry, but there was little he could do about it until they came upon a town. Besides, hunger was not new to him. Before he had found his family, he lived alone in the woods for a year, foraging for berries and nuts. He had not starved. One or two days without a proper meal would not kill him. Fire killed. Men killed. His own belly would not do him in.

He guessed he should have turned out Fowler's pockets. A dead man spends no coins. But that would have made him a thief indeed, and despite what Fowler had called him, he was none of that.

The road quite suddenly widened and ahead was the town. He recognized its gate. It seemed even grander than he remembered, made grander perhaps by his hunger and his fears. He let Goodie go her own pace, following after the wagons and carts, in through the stone gate marked with the town's seal. Gwethern.

Clearly it was a market day. Stalls lined the high street. There was more food—and more people—than Hawk had seen in a year. His stomach proclaimed his hunger loudly. But it proclaimed something else as well, a kind of ache that food would not take away. To buy food, he had to sell either Churn or Goodie, and they were his last ties to the farm. He got off the horse's back and led both horse and cow carefully through the crowded street.

Noise surrounded him: sellers calling out their wares, children whining for a sweet, women arguing over the price of a bit of cloth, a tinker bargaining with a man for a wild-eyed mare, a troubadour tuning his lute, two farmers arguing over stall space, and a general low hubbub.

For a boy used to living on a small quiet farm near a wood, it was suddenly too much, and Hawk backed up as if to escape it all, bumping into a barrow full of yellow apples.

"You! Boy!" came a shout from behind the barrow.

Hawk turned. There was a man with a face as yellow and sunken as any old apple; veins large as worm runnels crossed his nose.

Startled, Hawk stepped back against Goodie's shoulder and the man slammed a stick down across the barrow. If it had landed on Hawk, it would have been a sharp and painful blow.

"If you do not mean to buy, boy, you cannot touch."

"I . . . I . . ." Hawk began, suddenly remembering his strange dream about the apple.

"How do you know he does not mean to buy?" asked a voice behind him. Hawk was afraid to turn around in case the apple man struck out again, this time landing a blow.

"This rag of cloth hung on bones?" The apple cart man laughed. "He's no mother's son, by the dirt on him. A devil's spawn rather. Where would he get any coins?"

"You think he's a beggar? With that horse and cow?"

This time Hawk dared to look at his rescuer. The man was dressed in an outlandish blue cloak and feathered hat, like a mountebank.

"And as for that horse and cow . . ." the apple-faced man was saying, "where do you suppose he got them, the cheeky beggar."

"Right," the cloaked man said. "Cheeky indeed. And that's where he keeps his coin. In his cheek!" He laughed a sharp, yipping sound, which drew an appreciative chuckle from the crowd just starting to gather around them. Entertainment in any town being a rare commodity, even on market fair day, the folk of Gwethern were more than willing to egg on a fight.

"Open your mouth, boy, and give the man his coin."

Hawk was so surprised, his mouth dropped open on its own and a coin seemed to fall from his lips into the cloaked man's hand.

"Here," the man said, flipping the coin into the air. It turned twice over before the apple cart man grabbed it up, bit it, grunted, and shoved it into his purse.

The cloaked man picked out two yellow apples and placed one in each of Hawk's hands. As he did so, he whispered, "If you wish to repay me, boy, look for the green wagon, the castle on wheels."

Then he vanished into the crowd.

6. THE CASTLE
ON WHEELS

HAWK ATE THE TWO APPLES SLOWLY, SAVORING them. When he found a little green worm in the second one, he set the worm down carefully on a stone. It inched away, looking nothing at all like a dragon.

"Apples, worms . . . what does all this dreaming mean?" he asked himself aloud. Then he set out to look for the wagon.

It was not hard to find.

Parked under a chestnut tree, the wagon was as green as a fairy's gown. And it was indeed a castle on wheels, for the top of the wagon was vaulted over and an entire outline of a tower and keep was painted on the side. Hawk shivered. The dream, it seemed, was coming true.

Two docile, drab-colored mules were hitched to the wagon. They seemed oblivious to the sounds of the busy market day around them, contentedly nibbling on the few blades of brown grass that had managed to grow beneath the widespread tree.

Above the castle tower, on either side, were two painted figures. One was a tall, amber-eyed mage with a conical hat. The other was a dark-haired princess playing a harp.

Hawk walked quickly toward the wagon, pulling Goodie and Churn with him.

"So, boy, have you come to pay us back?" asked a soft voice. It was followed immediately by the trill of a mistle thrush.

At first he could not see who was speaking. Then something moved at one of the painted castle windows, a pale moon of a face. In a moment it had disappeared, and right after, a woman stepped through the castle door.

Hawk stared at her. She was possibly the most beautiful woman he had ever seen. She was not at all like Mag, who had been motherly and stout.

Or Nell, who had been all angles and elbows. Nor like any of the women dressed like crows in his dreams. There was not a woman he had seen at the market fair to compare with her. Her long dark hair, unbound, fell to her waist. She wore a dress of scarlet wool, and jewels in her ears that made a pleasant jangling, like a hawk's jesses. A yellow purse hung from a braided belt and it, too, jangled whenever she moved. As he watched, she bound up her hair with a single, swift motion into a net of scarlet linen.

She smiled. "Ding-dang-dong, cat's got your tongue, then?"

When he didn't answer, she laughed. But it wasn't a nasty laugh, at his expense. It was a laugh at the entire world, a laugh that invited him in. Before he could laugh back, though, she had reached back behind her and pulled out a harp, exactly like the one painted on the wagon's side. Strumming the harp with her long nails, she began to sing:

> "A boy with shirt a somber blue
> Will never ever come to rue,
> A boy with..."

"Are you singing about me?" asked Hawk, hoping she was.

"Do you think I am singing about you?" the woman asked, then pursed her lips and made the mistle thrush trill.

"If not now, you will someday," Hawk said. He did not know why he said it, but it seemed suddenly right, almost as if he had dreamed it.

"I believe you," said the woman, but she was busy tuning her harp at the same time. It was as if Hawk did not really exist for her except as an audience to be cozened. He was not sure he liked that.

Suddenly she stood. "You did not answer my question, boy."

"What question?"

"Have you come to pay what you owe?"

Puzzled, Hawk replied, "I did not answer because I did not know you were talking to me. I owe you nothing."

"Ah—but you owe it me," came a lower voice from inside the wagon, where it was dark. "And Viviane and I share all."

A man emerged from the wagon and, even

though he was not wearing the cloak, Hawk knew him. He was the mountebank, but he was also the mage on the wagon's side: the slate grey hair was the same. And the amber eyes.

"I do not owe you either, sir," Hawk said.

"What of the apples, boy? And the coin that fell from your mouth?"

Hawk looked straightaway into the man's eyes. "The coin was a trick. And the apples were meant to come to me, sir. I dreamed them."

The woman laughed. "Clever boy. And why did you come here to the green castle, if not to pay?" All the while she spoke, she smoothed her dress with her long slim fingers.

"As the apples were meant to come into my hands, so I believe I am to come into yours," Hawk said.

The woman laughed again, throwing her head back. The earrings and the purse jingled and jangled, as if they were laughing, too. "Only you hope," she said, suddenly quite serious, "that the mage will not eat you up and put your little green worm on a rock for some passing scavenger."

Hawk's mouth dropped open. "How did you know about the worm? About the dream?"

"Bards know everything," she said. "Everything about magic."

"And *tell* everything as well," said the mage. He clapped her lightly on the shoulder and she went, laughing and jangling, back through the wagon door.

7. THE MAGE

HAWK NODDED TO HIMSELF. "IT WAS THE WIN-
dow," he whispered at last, though the answer did
not entirely satisfy him.

"Of course it was the window," said the mage.
"And if you wish to speak to yourself so no one
else is the wiser, make it *sotto voce,* under the
breath thus." And while his lips moved, no sound
came out. "Still, a whisper is no guarantee of secrets," he laughed, "if there is one like my Viviane
who can read lips."

"*Sotto voce,*" Hawk said aloud. And then repeated, this time soundlessly.

"The soldiers first brought the phrase from far
Rome," the mage said. "But it rides the market

roads, now. Much that is knowledge came from there. Little grows in our land but oak and thorn."

"*Sotto voce*," Hawk repeated, punctuating his memory.

"I like you, boy," said the mage. "But then, I collect oddities."

"Did you collect the bard, sir?"

Looking quickly over his shoulder at the door into the wagon, the mage said, "Her?"

"Yes, sir."

"I did."

"How is—*she*—an oddity?" asked Hawk. "I think she is"—he took a gulp—"wonderful."

The mage smiled, as if he shared a joke with himself. "That she is. Quite wonderful, my Viviane. And well she knows it. She has a range of four octaves and can mimic any bird or beast I name." He paused. "And a few I cannot."

Hawk nodded solemnly. So solemnly, in fact, the mage laughed out loud. "You are an oddity, too, boy. I thought so when first I saw you riding through Gwethern gates, all raggedy and under-fed, yet like a prince on that plowhorse. Like a hero from one of the tales. 'There's one to watch!' I told myself."

"Sotto voce?" Hawk asked.

"Indeed. It is never good to let others in on one's secrets. So I followed you, asking about you in case there was someone who knew. But you were a mystery to everyone I asked. And then, when the apple man had at you, I saw my opportunity. You protested at neither the stick nor the coin dropping from your lips. I could feel your anger, your surprise. That calm, poised center—quite something in a boy your age. You *are* an oddity. I sniffed it out with my nose from the first. And my nose . . ." He tapped it with his forefinger, which made him look both wise and ominous at once. "My nose never lies. Do you think yourself odd?"

Hawk closed his eyes for a moment, thinking. When he opened them again, he said, "I have dreams."

The mage held his breath, a kind of innate wisdom on his part, and waited.

"I dreamed of a mage today. There was an apple and a worm in the dream as well. And a castle green as early spring grass. Now that I have seen your wagon, I know which castle. And I know you are the mage. And the green worm I myself placed upon the stone." He did not mention that it had become a dragon, thinking suddenly that it might be best to keep some of his dreaming *sotto voce*.

"Do you . . . dream . . . often?" the mage asked carefully, slowly coming down the steps of the wagon and sitting on the bottom step.

Hawk nodded.

"Tell me."

"You will think me a liar. Perhaps you will hit me," Hawk said.

This time the mage laughed out loud, with his head back, a low theatrical laugh, though Hawk —who knew nothing of the theater—did not know it as such. The mage stopped laughing and looked closely at the boy, narrowing his eyes. "I have never hit anyone in my life, boy. And telling lies is an essential part of magic. You lie with your hands, like this." So saying, he reached behind Hawk's ear and pulled out a bouquet of mead-owsweet, wintergreen, and a single blue aster. "You see—my hands told the lie that flowers grow in the dirt behind your ear. And your eyes believed it. And I know you have no mother, for there is no mother who would allow such dirt to remain for long on a boy's neck."

Hawk laughed at that until he almost cried.

The mage looked away to give him time to recover, then looked back. Then he leaned forward and whispered. "But never let Viviane know we tell lies. She is as practiced in her anger as she is on her harp. I may never swat a liar, but she is the very devil when her temper is aroused."

"I will not," Hawk said solemnly.

"Then tell me about your dreams."

He told them, then, one after another—the fire bird, the whistling priest, the bloodied man dead by the howling dog. The mage listened quietly, leaning forward every once in a while during the telling, as if by moving closer to the boy, he moved closer to an understanding of the dreams. And when Hawk was finished speaking, the mage reached over and clasped his hand tightly. Hawk felt something in his palm and looked down. It was a small copper coin.

"Buy yourself a meat pie, boy," the mage said. "And then come along with us. There is plenty of room in the green castle and I think you, your horse, and cow will make a fine addition to our traveling show."

"Thank you, sir," Hawk said.

"Not *sir*, for pity's sake. My name is Ambrosius, because of my amber eyes. Did you notice them? Ambrosius the Wandering Mage. It says so on the other side of the wagon, but I doubt you can read."

"I can, sir. Ambrosius." Hawk smiled shyly at this revelation.

"Ah," the man said, and squinted one eye as if reassessing the boy. "And what is your name? I cannot keep calling you boy."

Hawk hesitated, looking down.

"Come, come, I will not hit you. And you may keep the coin whatever you say. Names do not matter all that much now, do they?"

But the boy knew names *did* matter. Especially around power such as the mage's. He drew in a deep breath. "My name is Hawk," he said.

"Hawk is it?" Ambrosius smiled very carefully. "Well, perhaps someday you will grow into that name. And perhaps it is your real name. But caution dictates a change of nomenclature. For the road. You are a bit thin and undersized for a hawk. Even a young hawk."

A strange, sharp cackling sound came from the interior of the wagon, a high *ki-ki-ki-ki*.

Ambrosius looked back for a moment. "Viviane says you *are* a hawk, but a small one. A hobby, perhaps."

"Hobby," the boy whispered, knowing a hobby was still larger than a merlin. His hand clutched the coin so tightly it left a mark on his palm. "Hobby."

"Good. Then it is settled," Ambrosius said, standing. "Fly off to your meat pie, Hobby, then fly quickly back to me. We travel from here on to Carmarthen fair, a rather larger town for our playing. Viviane will sing like a lark. I will do my magic. And you—well, we will figure out something quite worthy, I can promise you. There are fortunes to be made on the road, young Hobby, if you can sing in four voices and pluck flowers out of the air."

8. THE CITY

THE ROAD WAS GENTLE AND WINDING, THROUGH still-green valleys and alongside clear, quick streams full of trout. The trees were green with touches of gold, but on the far ridges the forests were already bare. Days were growing shorter and overhead the greylags, in great vees, flew south amid a tremendous noise.

As the wagon bounced along, Viviane sang songs about Robin o' the Wood in a high, sweet voice, and about the Battle of the Trees in a voice that was low and thrilling. In a middle voice, rather like Hobby's own, she sang a lusty song about a bold warrior and a peasant maid that turned his cheeks pink and hot.

Ambrosius shortened the journey with his spirited tellings of wonder tales and histories, though which was which was sometimes hard to tell. There was the story of a wolf who suckled a pair of human twins, a great leader named Julius murdered by his friends, and another leader who had played on his lute while his city burned. This last was rather too close to Hobby's own history and he had to look away for a moment. When he looked back, it was to watch Ambrosius make coins walk across his knuckles. Then, almost as an afterthought, the mage reached into Hobby's shirt and drew out a turtledove. It surprised the bird even more than the boy, and the dove flew off onto a low branch of an ash tree and plucked at its feathers furiously until the wagon, trailing the horse and cow, had passed by.

They were two days traveling, wonderful days for Hobby. He felt content, caring little if they ever arrived at the city. At night he did not dream.

In between the two travel days, they spent one day resting the animals by a bright pond rimmed with willows.

"Carmarthen is over that hill," Ambrosius said, pointing. "But it will wait. The fair is not for two days yet. Viviane has costumes to tidy and we, my boy, we have fishing. A man—whether a mage or a murderer—can always find time to fish."

He took Hobby down to the pond and there, Ambrosius proved himself a bad angler but a merry companion. All he managed to catch was one angry turtle, but the stories he told until dark more than made up for his incompetence. It was Hobby who pulled in the one small spotted trout they roasted over the fire that night and shared three ways.

"Did you know," Ambrosius said as they banked the fire, "that the Celts in Eire believe little spotted fish can rise up out of the water prophesying? Who knows what this one might have told us."

Viviane suddenly burst in with a bubbly song:

> "The warrrrrrrrrrrters are cold,
> But crystal clearrrrrrrr;
> I rrrrrrrise to the fly
> And so appearrrrrrr . . ."

"You appear to be interrupting the story," Ambrosius said, and they all laughed.

"Hobby, take these plates to the stream and rinse them. This old man needs to be taught his manners," Viviane said.

Hobby took the plates and went down to the stream. With his hands in the cold water, he began to dream. It was a dream in which he was a child again, with a mother and father rocking him to sleep, the *creak-creak-creak* of the cradle sounding suspiciously like the wheels of the green castle cart.

When he woke, his hands were like ice, and an almost full moon was reflected in silver shards in the water.

Theirs was not the only wagon on the road before dawn, but it was the gaudiest by far. Peddlers' children leaped off their own wagons to run alongside, begging the magician for a trick. He did one for each child and asked for no coins at all, even though Viviane scolded about it.

"Each child will bring another to us," he said, "once we are in the town. They will be our best criers. And those who come in Carmarthen will not get away free." He made a showy pink musk mallow appear from under the chin of a dirt-faced tinker girl, this trick even more remarkable—thought Hobby—because musk mallow was long past season. The girl giggled, took the flower, and ran off.

Viviane shook her head. It was clearly an old argument between them.

At first each trick made Hobby gasp with delight. At twelve he was still child enough to be guiled. But partway through the day he began to notice where the flowers and scarves and eggs really appeared from—out of the vast sleeves of the mage's robe. He started watching Ambrosius' hands carefully through slotted eyes and, unconsciously, began to imitate him.

Viviane reached over and slapped his fingers so hard they burned. "Here!" she said sharply. "It is bad enough he does tricks for free on the road, but you would beggar us for sure if you give his secrets away."

So, Hobby thought, *there are secrets of the hand as well as the tongue. Sotto voce, indeed.* He was both embarrassed and elated by Viviane's attention, and by his discovery. And, to be truthful, a bit upset that the mage's magic had less to do with some real power and more to do with imag-ination. Still, his quiet concentration on the mage's tricks and the constant rocking of the wagon soon combined to put him to sleep. Again he dreamed. It was a wicked, nasty dream in which Viviane was as young as he and a white-thorn tree fell upon her. When he awoke, he was suddenly afraid that the dream would come true. He wanted to warn her, but then remembered that his dreams did not seem to come true liter-ally, but only *on the slant*. It would do no good to tell her if he did not understand the dream. That thought lent him a small amount of comfort.

If Gwethern had been a bustling little market town, Carmarthen had to be the very center of the commercial world. As they neared it, Hobby saw gardens and orchards laid out in careful squares outside the towering city walls. Some of the trees along the northern edges were ruined, the ground around them raw and wounded. There were spotty pastures where sheep and kine grazed on the fall stubble. The city walls were made up of large blocks of limestone, though who could have moved such giant stones was a mystery to him. Above the walls he glimpsed crenellated towers from which red and white banners waved gaudily in the shifting winds.

Unable to contain himself any longer, Hobby scrambled through the door of the wagon and squeezed in between Ambrosius and Viviane.

"Look!" he cried.

Viviane smiled at the childish outburst, but Ambrosius shook his head. "Not enough just to look, my boy," he said. "You must use all your senses here if we are to prosper. The eyes and ears are different listeners, but both feed into magecraft."

Viviane rolled her eyes up. "What makes an old man want to *lecture* all the time?" she said, not quite to herself.

Ambrosius ignored her. "What do you hear?"

Once Hobby had been used to listening, the year he had been alone in the woods. He had listened for danger: for the sound of dog and bear and wolf. He had listened for changes in the weather: leaves rustling, the grumble of the sky. And then for four years he had learned to listen to the sounds of the farm—to the needs of dogs and hens, horse and cows, and to make out the

9. SECRETS

IN A SUIT OF GREENS AND GOLDS—THE GOLD a cotta of the mage's that Viviane had tailored to fit him, the green some old hose sewn over with gold patches and bells—Hobby strode through the crowd with a tambourine collecting coins after each performance.

"Our boy Hobby will pass amongst you, a small hawk among the pigeons," Ambrosius had announced before completing his final trick, the one in which Viviane was shut up in a box and subsequently disappeared, appearing again with a great flourish at the wagon's door.

Hobby had glowed when Ambrosius pronounced his name and claimed, aloud, possession of him. *Our* boy, the mage said, as if they were a family, just the three of them. As in his dream. Hobby repeated the phrase *sotto voce* and smiled. That infectious smile brought coins waterfalling into his tambourine, though he was unaware of its power.

On the third day of the fair, after their evening performance, when Viviane had sung in three different voices at the wagon's door, a broad-faced soldier with a red plume came up to them and stood carefully at attention.

He waited for the crowd to dissipate, then announced to Ambrosius: "The Lady Renwein would have you come this evening to the old palace and sends this purse by way of a promise. There will be more if the performance is satisfactory." He dropped the purse into Ambrosius' hand.

The mage bowed low and then, with a wink at Hobby, began drawing out a series of colored scarves from behind the soldier's ear. They were all shades of red: crimson, pink, vermillion, flame, scarlet, carmine, and rose.

"For your lady," he said to the soldier.

The soldier relaxed, laughed, and took them. "They are her colors. She will be pleased. Though not, I think, his lordship."

"The white soldiers are his, then?" asked Ambrosius.

The soldier grunted. It was all the answer he gave. "Be in the kitchen for dinner. You shall eat what the cook eats."

"Then let us hope," Viviane said, taking the purse from Ambrosius' hand, "that we like what the cook likes."

They packed up all they would need for the performance in two large baskets and walked toward the old palace at six of the clock, the bells ringing out the hour.

Along the wall of the old palace were ranged guards in pairs, one red and one white. Ambrosius pulled on his beard thoughtfully.

"Hobby," he asked, "when you went through the fair between our performances, did you hear any of the guards talking?"

"Not talking exactly," Hobby said. "But matching names."

"What names?"

"The red guards called the white guards things like 'Dirty Men of a Dirty Duke.'"

"And the white?"

"Must I say?" Hobby asked. "It touches on the lady's reputation."

"You must," the mage answered. "What touches her, may touch us."

"She was called Dragonlady."

"Ah," Viviane said. "And that is no good thing? I have been called worse in my time." She laughed.

Hobby felt his cheeks sting with embarrassment. "And the red guards called the Duke 'Draco.' Two dragons in the same nest might make for a difficult marriage."

"A difficult performance for us at any rate," Ambrosius said. "But hush. We near the palace gate."

10. THE PLAYERS

THE CASTLE WAS INDEED OLD. ITS KEEP, FROM the time of the Romans, stood mottled and pocked. The newer parts of the building, while colorful, were of shoddy material and worse workmanship. Ambrosius remarked on it quietly as they passed along the corridors.

"The sounds of construction we heard are not from here but for a brand-new castle," he said. "One hopes it is better built than this."

But when they reached the kitchen, the cook —with a stomach as round as a drum and a mouth that seemed always open—told them how badly that building was going. "The lady's father, the old Duke, fair beggared us fighting off imagined invaders. But then he married off his daughter to the worst invader of all, a man who fancies himself king. At least the Romans knew how to build roads and baths. We still use those that stand. But now..." He made the sign of horns with his right hand and spat through his fingers to ward off bad luck. "Now the countryside's in tatters from armies marching through; and the crops are hardly planted before they're thrashed down by the horses; and the new Duke making it worse building a great new house on the site of the old Roman barracks."

Viviane appeared not to listen but Ambrosius urged the cook on to more revelations. Hobby stopped attending after a while and turned his mind to the food, which was plentiful and rich. He ate so much he nearly made himself sick and curled, like a dog, three times around before settling on a cushion near the hearth. The cook's voice followed him where he lay.

"The foundation doesn't hold. What is built up by day falls down by night," the cook was saying as Hobby drifted into sleep.

A hand on his shoulder roused him, though he was still partially within his dream.

"The dragons..." he murmured, opening his eyes.

"Hush," Ambrosius said. "Hush, my boy, and remember. You called out many times in your sleep—of dragons and castles, water and blood. Remember the dream and I will tell you when to spin out the tale of it to catch the conscience of Carmarthen in its web. If I am right, there will be many coins in this." He winked and touched his finger to his nose.

Hobby closed his eyes and forced himself to remember every inch of the dream. Suddenly his hair was pulled. "Ow!" he cried, opening his eyes again.

"You are a sight!" Viviane said. "A smudge on your cheek from the hearth cushion and hair in tangles. Let me comb it." And without waiting for permission, she began running her comb through his hair.

He let her do it, of course, but it bothered him, so he tried to concentrate instead on the incredible bustle of the kitchen. The cook was now too busy to gossip with them, working at the fire: basting, stirring, turning the spit, calling out a string of instructions to his overworked crew.

"Stephen—here—more juice. Wine up to the tables and hurry, Beth, Mavis, Gwen! They are pounding their feet on the floor. That's not a good sign. The soup is hot enough—run the tureens up, and mind the handles! Use a cloth, Nan, stupid girl! And where are the sharp knives? These be dull as Saxon wit. David—step lively! The pies must come out of the oast now or they burn!"

Ambrosius stood in a corner, well away from the busyness, limbering up his fingers. Viviane began tuning her harp, concentrating with a passionate intensity that shut out everything else.

"Come, mage."

Hobby turned at the voice. It was the same soldier who had brought them to the castle, his broad, homely face now split with a smile, wine having worked its own magic.

"Come, mage. And you, singer. Her ladyship asks you to begin."

Ambrosius pointed to his baskets of apparatus. "Will you bring them up?"

Grunting, the soldier returned to his earlier gruff form, but hefted the baskets anyway. "Why not have the boy carry and fetch?"

"He can carry if he has to," Ambrosius said, "but he is much more to us than that."

The soldier laughed. "You will have no use for a tambourine boy here."

Ambrosius stood very still, letting his voice drop to a low whisper. "I have performed in higher courts than this. I know what is fit for fairs and what is fit for the Great Hall. The boy does not spill out his tricks for peasants." He moved to Hobby's side and put a hand on the boy's shoulder. "He is a reader of dreams. What he dreams comes true."

"Is that so?" the soldier asked all of them.

"It is so," Viviane said, smiling at him intimately.

Hobby closed his eyes for a moment, and when he opened them again they were the color of an ocean swell. "It *is* so."

11. DREAM-READER

VIVIANE SANG FIRST, A MEDLEY OF LOVE SONGS that favored the Duke and his lady equally. Such was her ability that each took the songs as flattering, though Hobby thought he detected a nasty undertone that made him uncomfortable. But Viviane was roundly applauded.

Deftly beginning his own performance at the moment Viviane ended hers, even cutting into her applause, Ambrosius started with silly tricks. He plucked eggs, coins, even a turtle from behind an unsuspecting soldier's ear. Hobby recognized the turtle; it was the one Ambrosius had caught when they were fishing.

Then the mage moved on to finer tricks, like guessing the name of a soldier's sweetheart, or discovering the missing red queen from a card deck under the Lady Renwein's plate. Finally he made Viviane disappear and reappear in a series of boxes, the last of which he had the soldiers thrust through with their swords. The final trick caused the soldiers much consternation, for blood appeared to leak from the boxes, though it was—Hobby knew—juices from the meat they'd had for dinner, which Viviane had kept concealed in a flask.

When she was revealed whole and hale, the hall resounded with huzzahs. The Duke smiled, whispering to Lady Renwein. She covered his hand with hers and when he withdrew his hand he held a plump purse, which he jangled at them.

"We are pleased to offer you this, mage."

"Thank you, my lord," said Ambrosius, "but we are not done yet. I would introduce you to my boy Hobby, who will tell you of a singular dream he had this day."

Hobby was led by the mage into the very center of the room. His legs trembled, but the mage whispered to him, "Do not be afraid. Simply tell the dream. Leave the rest to me."

Hobby nodded, closed his eyes as if he

dreamed still, and began. "I dreamed a tower of snow that in the day reached as high as the sky but at night melted to the ground."

"The castle!" the Duke gasped, but Lady Renwein placed her hand once more on his.

"Hush, my lord," she whispered. "This is a magician's trick. They have been in Carmarthen these three days and surely they have heard of it. It is hardly a secret."

Eyes closed, Hobby seemed not to hear them but continued on. "And then a man—a mage I think—advised them that the melted water left in the morning should be drained away. It was done as he wished, though the soldiers complained bitterly of it. At last the pool was gone and there in the mud lay two great stones, round and speckled as eggs.

"Then the mage drew a sword and struck open the eggs. In one was a dragon the color of wine, in the other a dragon the color of maggots."

There was a collective gasp from the audience, but Hobby could not stop speaking. It was as if a fever had hold of him.

"When the two dragons saw they were revealed," he said, "they turned not on the soldiers nor on the mage, but on one another. Screaming and breathing fire in the mud, they rose into the air belching smoke. At first the white had the best of it, then the red, turning over and over in the lightening sky. At last with a final clash, breast against breast, the white gashed a great hole in the red's neck and it tumbled end over end down to defeat."

At that, Hobby opened his eyes and they were the sudden green of gooseberries.

The Lady Renwein's face looked dark and disturbed. "What does that dream mean, boy?"

Ambrosius stepped between Hobby and the high table. "The boy dreams, my lady, but leaves it to me to make sense of his dreams, just as did his dear, dead mother before him."

Startled, Hobby turned to Viviane. She rolled her eyes up at the ceiling and held her mouth still.

"His mother was a dream-reader, too?" the Duke asked.

"She was," Ambrosius said, "though being a woman she dreamed of more homey things: the names of babes, the color of their eyes, and whether they be boys or girls."

Lady Renwein leaned forward. "Then say what this dream of towers and dragons means, mage."

"I will, my lady. It is of course not unknown to us that you have a house that will not stand. All the town speaks of it. However, our young Hobby has dreamed the reason for the failure. The house does not stand—in dream images it melts—because there is a pool beneath it, most likely a conduit that the Romans built for their baths. With your construction there has been leakage underground. Open the foundation of your house, drain the pool, remove or reconstruct the Roman pipes, and the building will remain whole."

"Is that all?" The Duke sounded disappointed. "I thought you might say that the red dragon was the lady's and the white mine, or some such."

"Dreams are devious, my lord," Ambrosius said, putting his hand once again on Hobby's shoulder. "Truth on the slant."

But Lady Renwein was nodding. "Yes, that makes sense, about the conduits and the drain. You need not have done all this folderol with dreams in order to give us good advice."

Ambrosius smiled, stepped away from Hobby, and bowed deeply. "But, my lady, would you have listened to a traveling magician on matters of . . . state?"

Lady Renwein smiled back, a look of perfect understanding passing between them.

"Besides," Ambrosius said, "I had not heard the boy's dream till this very moment. The cook will vouch for that. Nor have I given thought to your new home or anything else in Carmarthen, excepting the fair. It was the boy's dream that instructed us in what must be done. Like his mother, of blessed memory. She, the minx, never mentioned she was carrying a boy. Though when she had him, she said, 'He will be a hawk among princes.' And thus saying, she died. So I named him Hobby. A small hawk, but mine own."

At that Hobby started. All this talk of mothers had merely irritated him. But the fact that Ambrosius called him "mine own" made him flush with a combination of pride and embarrassment. Was there *nothing* the mage would not say for a prize?

12. A DIFFERENT READING

IT WAS TWO DAYS LATER THAT A MESSENGER arrived at the green wagon with a small casket full of coins as well as a small gold dragon pendant with a faceted red jewel for an eye.

"Her ladyship sends these with her compliments," the messenger said. "There was indeed a hidden pool beneath the foundation. And the pipes, which were grey and speckled as eggs, were rotted clear through. The Duke begs you to stay for yet another dream. He says the boy is indeed a hawk among princes."

Ambrosius smiled. "Thank them both from us and say that we will let the boy dream tonight and come tomorrow with him."

After the messenger had departed, Viviane laughed. "Hawk among princes indeed!" She ran her fingers through the coins. "Here, hawkling," she said, placing the pendant's chain over Hobby's head.

The thing lay like a cold supper on his stomach and he shivered. He had been thinking for two days about all the lies Ambrosius had told the Duke, one atop another. Yet some were lies even he wanted to believe in. A mother and father who loved him and named him. How could he be angry with the mage when that was what he most desired? Still, he had to say it, had to ask.

"You made it all up," he said. There was accusation in his voice and—to be truthful—a bit of a whine. Twelve years was not yet too old for whining. "About my mother. About the dream."

"About your mother, yes," Ambrosius admitted. "But not the dream."

"You lied."

Viviane shrugged and picked up the casket of coins. "And what of that? All magecraft is a lie," she said. "All performance. A lie, if done well, becomes truth." She placed the casket under an embroidered cloth.

"No lie in *her* performance that night," said Ambrosius. "Did you see how she managed them?" He blew her a kiss.

Viviane came over to him and touched his cheek fondly.

Hobby felt cold. They seemed quite giddy with themselves. "But you lied about the dream. It meant *nothing* like that." He wondered how he knew such a thing, but it was as if he suddenly had been given a gift of understanding simply by mentioning the dream. "Nothing."

"What do you mean?" Ambrosius asked cautiously. There was a slyness—and a fear—in his eyes that he could not disguise.

Hobby weighed his words carefully. He thought his entire future might lie in what he said next. "The dream, Ambrosius. It was not about drains."

"Ah . . ." Ambrosius let out only one small syllable.

"It was a dream about . . . armies, about the Duke's losses to come. There will be a battle, and his army will be defeated. He was right in a way. And you dismissed him."

"I did not dismiss him," Ambrosius said. "I side-stepped him. To tell a prince to his face that you have dreamed his doom invites your own. The greatest wisdom of any dreamer is to live to dream again." He smiled, but it sat on his mouth and never reached his eyes. Unaccountably his brow was spotted with sweat.

"The only duty of the dreamer is to tell the truth," Hobby said. "About the dream."

"You do not listen well," Viviane said.

"*He* does not listen at all," Hobby retorted, suddenly sure that Ambrosius had never understood the dream's meaning. The man was a charlatan through and through. The actual dream had never mattered. He would have told the Duke the same whatever the dream. Lady Renwein had the right of it. And Hobby suddenly knew something else as well: Ambrosius was afraid of both the dream and the dreamer. "You are jealous and afraid," he spat out. "You know yourself to be nothing more than a sleight-of-hander. *I* am the true dream-reader."

Ambrosius did not answer, his face drawn.

"I am sorry," Hobby said quickly. "I should not have said that." But whether he meant he was sorry for his tongue's sharpness or for saying out loud what they all already knew, none of them was sure.

Ambrosius turned and gave Viviane an unreadable look. "The boy is right about one thing. My hand is quicker than my mind. We go from here at once."

"Tomorrow is soon enough."

"Now."

"Boy," Viviane said, turning a smile on Hobby that made him flush all over. "Take these coins. Go into town. Buy yourself some token of the place. Kiss a pretty wench. Twelve years is none too soon for that." She reached into the pocket that hung from her belt and fetched out a handful of coins, much too much for an evening's entertainment. "Come back in an hour or two. No sooner. I will change this stubborn old man's mind that we all may have a good night's rest."

Hobby took the coins and went. Not to buy a token. Not to kiss a town maid. But to think long and hard about the power he had, this dreaming. And to think what it had to do with the matter of truth.

13. RESURRECTION

THE TOWN WAS QUIET, THE STALLS SHUT DOWN, the players all in their beds. The tubs and trestles on which goods had stood all day were pulled in for the night.

Hobby wandered through the empty town, sitting at last with his back to a stone watering trough, meaning to think. Instead he fell asleep and dreamed.

He dreamed three dreams. The first was of a hand pushing up through earth, as if someone long buried sought the light. A revenant, a shadow, a ghost to haunt him. He cried out and his own cry wakened him for a moment.

The second dream was not so frightening as the first. There was a bear, not much more than a cub, padding through the woods with a crown upon its head.

The third was a dream of a tree and in the dream he slept, dreaming.

A rough hand shook him awake. He swam up into the light of the torch, thinking, *It will be one of the guards. Or Ambrosius. Or Viviane,* though the touch was too rough for hers.

But when he heard the low, familiar growl of a dog, he knew that his first dream had, in its own way, come true. "Fowler," he whispered, meaning both the man and his breath. "I thought you were dead."

"You left me unconscious, boy. And we such good friends," Fowler said. "I heard about you when I arrived. Quite a performance, I was told. The Duke wants more. He's not yet satisfied."

"How did you know it was me?"

"Oh, a duke's spy has his little ways." The man laughed. "But a strange boy with eyes like gooseberries was a sign. That horse and cow a surety. You picked my pocket."

"I never . . ." Hobby's voice was more vehement than an innocent's should have been. It was because he *had* considered—if only for a moment—stealing from the foul man.

"At least you left me my boots."

"Master Robin's boots, you mean."

"Master Robin, is it? I heard his name was Ambrosius. He has as many names as you, young Hawk." Fowler smiled. In the torchlight his one good eye gleamed, the scarred eye was black as an empty socket. "I shall have to speak to your master for recompense. He took my boy, my horse, my cow. He shall have to pay me or I take it out in blood. Your blood for mine. Blood, they say, makes great bargains."

Hobby twisted in the man's hand but could not shake his hold. The dog growled.

"Up, hawkling." He yanked the boy to his feet and they marched through the shadows toward the castle on wheels.

But the green wagon was gone. Gone were the mules. And gone as well were Goodie and Churn.

Hobby wrenched free of Fowler's hand, scouring the darkness. But he did not bother to call out. He knew, from the hard stone sitting in his chest, that they had fled long since, taking his horse and cow with them. All he had of them, his new family, was the Lady Renwein's pendant and a handful of coins. Viviane had not overpaid him after all.

The chapel bell tolled midnight and Hobby willed himself not to cry.

"So they have flown the dovecote, leaving the little pigeon behind," Fowler said, his hand once more heavy on Hobby's shoulder.

Hobby did not bother to answer. Indeed, what could he have said? That he had been cozened by Viviane's smile and an evening's worth of coppers? That he had believed Ambrosius wanted him for a son? That they had run off in the end because they were afraid of him, afraid of his dreaming?

"I wonder the Duke let them go," Fowler mused aloud. "But perhaps he does not know they are gone yet. Perhaps they greased the palm of some willing gatekeeper. There may be some good to be made from this yet."

"You mean good for *you*," Hobby said.

"That is all anyone ever means, boy," Fowler said. He laughed out loud and at that his dog slapped at the ground with a paw. Neither sound was comforting. "Come, Hawk. I expect the Duke would like to know that you, at least, are safe and awake."

14. TRUE MAGIC

THEY WENT UP TO THE DUKE'S PRIVATE APART-
ments by a twisting back stair. At each turning
stood a stone-eyed guard, hand on sword beneath
a flickering wall torch. The flames made shadows
crawl up and down the stairs. Hobby could not
have run, even if he dared, not because of the
guards but because Fowler's hand was ever on his
shoulder.

The Duke was waiting for them, sitting at a
great desk near a window. He was fingering pa-
pers and his eyes were not on them. Hobby could
not tell if the man was just tired or if he—like
most of the nobles—was unlettered. His eyes,
however, were on Hobby and his keeper, and
these two he could read very well indeed.

"You have brought me the singing bird but not his handler," the Duke said. "He is no good to me without his quick-fingered interpreter, that mage."

Hobby spoke up at once. If Fowler had hoped to get something for his news, he would not. "The mage, Ambrosius, is gone. You will not find him."

"A father desert his child?" the Duke asked, then gave a short laugh, musing aloud. "The forest teems with such leavings—boys and girls without hope of family or life. Why should *your* father be different?"

Hobby looked down at the rushes on the floor. "He is *not* my father. My father was a falconer." Then he looked up, staring directly into the Duke's eyes. "Ambrosius is no real magic maker either."

The Duke leaned back in his chair and made a triangle of his fingers. "A charlatan. And you think this news surprises me?" But his face spoke differently.

Fowler chuckled.

"Are you a charlatan, too, boy?" the Duke asked.

"I do not know what I am," Hobby answered truthfully, for his magic required it.

"Are your dreams trickery then?" The Duke was like a hound on a scent.

Hobby suddenly remembered Ambrosius' warning against speaking truth to princes. Yet he knew, in his very bones, that he had to answer all direct questions of his magic directly. "My dreams come true. But on the slant."

"On the slant." The Duke closed his eyes and his voice was old. "I am not a man of such angles," he said. "We have got already what we wanted from the mage. The building stands. What more I seek, I do not rightly know. Can you tell me more, boy?"

The question was specific and Hobby knew he had no choice but to speak the truth. "There is more, sir."

"Then tell it me," the Duke said, with a sigh.

"The dragons are meant to be armies." Hobby spoke quietly but not so quietly that he could not be heard in that hush of a room. "Not your army or your wife's. But greater armies than both. There will be a battle and you will have the worst of it."

"How much worse?"

Hobby drew in a breath. He could not stop telling the dream. "You will die. Burned up in flame greater than dragon's breath."

"What battle, boy?" Fowler asked. "When?" He had drawn close to Hobby's side and breathed the questions into the boy's ear.

"My dream does not name a time or place of battle," Hobby said.

"Then, boy," the Duke said, "your dream is useless. I dream every night of battles. Some I win, some I lose. In this world there are always battles. There are always deaths. When you are a duke. When you would be a king." He stood and turned his back on the boy and the spy, staring out through the window to the blackness beyond. "I am not afraid to die cleanly, on the battlefield. But burning..." He shuddered. "I do not believe your slantwise dreaming. It is too tricky for an old soldier. Go away, boy. You tire me." And indeed the Duke's shoulders seemed to sag and his voice was ragged, as if torn on a nail.

"But perhaps..." Fowler began.

The Duke turned around abruptly, suddenly years younger in his fury. "But me no buts, Master

Mind-It-All. You have brought me no news from the south. No news about my enemies, about the numbers of their armies, about where they march and when. You have brought me only a charlatan, long fled, and a boy who dreams—so he says— my death by burning. *Burning!* Like a common witch. Like a warlock. *I will not hear of it.*" He glared at Fowler and not at Hobby. If he had looked at the boy, his story might have ended differently. But he did not. He concentrated all his anger on the man opposite him. "I will not be fooled. I am a fighting man. I do not listen to the dreams of ragged boys. Run along, child, and find your father. If you can."

Hobby turned to leave and the dog, who had been lying at Fowler's feet, rose and walked stiff-legged toward him, the hair on the ridge of its neck rising.

"I do not believe he is an ordinary boy, my lord," Fowler said. "Neither does my dog. He is more than the son of a falconer or the boy of a wandering player. I believe we need to find out *who* he is. Test his magic. Then perhaps he will be able to tell us the time and place of battles, the time and place of . . ."

"Of my death?" The fury in the Duke's voice was controlled now, tight, and the more dangerous for it. "So you can sell that piece of information to someone else?"

"My lord, do you so mistrust me?" Fowler asked.

"You have asked too many wrong questions already and not enough right ones," the Duke said. "I would be a fool *not* to mistrust you. I am no fool."

"Just his name, my lord duke," Fowler said. But he asked it of the Duke, not Hobby.

Hobby hesitated, knowing that names held power. Though he had not been asked directly, and though it was not about a dream, it still touched on his magic. But not—he realized—directly. "I am a hawk," he said, humor hidden in his answer. "A hawk among princes."

The Duke laughed explosively as if he got the joke. "A hawk. Ah yes, I remember your name now, Hobby. Fly away, little hawk, before I change my mind."

"Hawk," said Fowler, remembering the other name, and reaching for the boy.

"Merlin," the boy whispered, but *sotto voce*,

without sound. Then, as the Duke had ordered, he flew back down the stairs and out into the night, where armies were, truly, massing on the far side of the woods.

He flew unerringly into those woods, and freedom.

Light.

Morn.

"What is that hawk, Viviane? The one circling above us. Is it a hobby?"

"There is no hawk above us, old man. There is only cloud and, beyond it, sky."

"I heard the hawk. I heard his voice."

"It was a dream."

"I never dream. Only he dreams."

"You will dream a long dream soon. About the times when your fingers were swift and sure with magic. When you could pluck asters and asphodels from a child's ear."

"I never could do magic. Not like the boy."

"Hush. There was no boy. That was only a dream. Drink this and the dream will come again. For good."

The bells in her earrings ring like the sound of a tamed hawk's jesses, like the sound of a freed soul as it makes its long and perilous passage between earth and heaven.

MERLIN

Merlin:
The smallest British falcon or hawk,
its wingbeats are powerful and,
despite its size, it seldom fails of its prey.

Dark.

Night.

"It is your turn, Green Man. Set down your cards."

"I have you beaten, little bear. I hold a ten and a face."

"You have cheated."

"I never cheat."

"Except when it pleases you."

"You do not believe me, child?"

"I believe you have a ten and a face. But of what suit? Flowers? Game birds? Or the wild men of the woods? If they do not match, Green Man, I will beat you yet."

"You think too much on winning. On losing. Child, this is a game."

"I like games, Green Man. I am good at them."

"Being good at games should not be your only goal. You must think on other things. There is more to becoming an adult than games."

"Then I do not wish to become an adult. I wish to remain a child and play games. I am good at them."

"Such cannot be. The world grows old, and we with it. All life turns on the great wheel: dark to light to dark again."

"Can you not change that, magic maker?"

"Even I cannot."

"Then what will be left of childhood when we are grown old and gone?"

"Dreams are left, child. Dreams."

"I do not want to be someone else's dream, Green Man. I mean to stay awake."

Light.

Day.

1. FLIGHT

PURSUED BY DREAMS, THE BOY FLED FROM the town. They were not his dreams; they were the town's dreams, rough and hot and angry and full of blood.

He squirmed through a bolt-hole in the stone walls, a hole big enough for a badger or fox. Though twelve years old, he was a small boy and he just managed to fit. Sliding down the grassy embankment, he kept an eye out for the green wagon in which his family—or at least all the family he could claim—had left the town hours earlier.

But as it was night, he somehow got on the

wrong path, and he did not come upon any sign of them. Not the wagon which—even in the dark—would have been unmistakable as it was painted and shaped to look like a castle on wheels. Nor the man who claimed to be his father but was not. Nor the woman who made no such claims. Nor the mules who pulled, nor the horse and cow.

He was on his own. He was alone.

Everything, he thought wildly, *everything conspires to keep me on my lone.* By this he meant he could not go back into the town because of the dreams and because the lord of the town, Duke Vortigern, had told him to go. And because the Duke's own spy, a man named Fowler, hated him and would make him a prisoner if he could. And Fowler's even fouler dog knew his scent and would savage him on command.

And by this the boy also meant that the man in the wagon, Ambrosius, feared the boy's powers, and his woman agreed. They had run not from the Duke's anger but from their own fear.

"I shall have to go into the woods," the boy told himself.

The woods did not frighten him. The entire year he was eight, he had lived abandoned in the forest by himself. He had lived as a wild boy, a *wodewose*, without clothing, without warm food, or bedding, or the comfort of story or song. Without words. Without memory. But he had survived it till tamed by Master Robin, a falconer, and in Master Robin's house given a name and a history.

Surely, he thought, *I can do at twelve what I did at eight.*

But it was the middle of the night, and a forest—even one you know—can be a fearsome place. So he picked out a tree not too deep into the woods, an oak with a tall, ragged crown which he could just make out against the starry sky. It was a sturdy tree, its trunk wider than he could comfortably span with his arms, with a ridged bark that made it easy to climb.

He settled into the V-shaped crotch of the tree, some ten feet off the ground, certain he would be safe there from fox and wolf. Then, pulling his knees up to his chest, he slept.

And dreamed.

He dreamed about a bear in the forest. A bear

with a gold coronet on its head. A bear that walked upright, like a man.

A bear!

In his dream he crossed his fingers, an old trick of his that forced him to wake. Shivering in the dark, he drew his legs up even closer. He had found over the years that his dreams had an uncanny way of coming true, but on the slant. A bear—even slantwise—was a danger. It had teeth and claws. It could climb a tree.

But the bear in his dream had not seemed particularly menacing. It had not even been more than a cub. Besides, the dream was an old one he had had before, and he had yet to see a bear when he was awake, except for one old ratty creature leashed to a traveler that danced to the sad pipings of a flute at the fair. So settling deeper into the curve of the trunk, he slept again.

This time he did not dream.

Birdsong woke him, a blend of thrush and willow tit and the harsh *kraah kraah* of the hoodie crow. His legs were cramped, his shoulders aching, but he was alive. And it was day.

He put his head back and sang:

In the woods, in the woods,
My dear-i-o,
Where the birds, the birds sing
Cheer-i-o...

It was all he could remember of a song that Viviane, the woman in the green wagon, had sung once. But even so it gave him heart. He jumped down from the tree, found a stream, and washed his hands and face in the cold water. It was a habit left over from his first family, Master Robin's family.

Thinking about them made him think as well of the man Fowler and his dog who might at any moment be on his trail. Fowler was not the kind of man who slept late or gave up easily.

It should have made the boy afraid, but for some reason it did not. He began singing again as he struck off even more deeply into the woods.

2. FISHING

THE DEEPER HE WENT INTO THE WOODS, the more there were shadows. Overhead, the interlaced branches made a kind of roof that the sun only occasionally broke through. Ahead of him a red butterfly flitted over fallen leaves, settling at last on a patch of ivy. By the side of the path, bittersweet berries were already half changed from green to scarlet and the flooring of bracken was an autumnal copper brown. He liked the sound his feet made as he walked, a soft crunching.

Turning his face toward the yellowing tree roof, he drew in a deep breath. He should have been worried about where his next meal would come from or that Fowler would find him. He should have worried about the dream bear. But somehow here, in the heart of the woods, he felt secure.

Just then he heard the nearby sound of water over stone. Following the sound he came to a small river winding between willows. There was a large grey rock half in and half out of the water and he sat upon it to rest. It was smooth and cool; he liked the feel of it. When he leaned over to look into the water, he was startled by a silvery flash.

Fish, his conscious mind told him. But as he continued staring at its sinuous movement, he became mesmerized, and suddenly he found himself *in* the water, swimming by the fish's side. Overhead, light filtered through the river's ceiling in a shower of golden shards.

The boy swam nose to tail with the trout, following it into deeper and deeper waters where the sunlight could not penetrate. Yet, oddly, he could still see clearly in the blue-green of the river morning.

He did not question that he could breathe

under the water; indeed it seemed as natural to him as breathing air.

Little tendrils of plants, like the touch of soft fingers, brushed by him. Smaller fish darted at the edges of his sight. Then nose to tail, he and the trout traveled even further down into the depths of the darkening pool.

The trout was thick along its back and covered with a shimmer of silver marked with black spots and crosses, like a shield. As it swam, it browsed on tiny shrimp, a moveable feast. Then, suddenly, it turned and stared at him with one bold eye.

"Do not rise to the lure, lad," it said in a voice surprisingly chesty and deep. Bubbles fizzed from its mouth like punctuation. Then it was gone in a flurry of waves, so fast the boy could not follow. He blinked, and once more found himself sitting upon the rock, completely dry.

"That was not exactly a dream," he whispered to himself. But he knew it was not exactly real either. Still, the shards of filtered light through water, the silver back of the trout, its resonant voice had seemed all too true.

"Do not rise to the lure," he repeated quietly, glancing around at the forest. But seeing nothing that looked the least like a lure, he stood, brushed himself off, and headed deeper into the woods.

3. THE PACK

HE PUZZLED OVER HIS ADVENTURE WITH
the trout for hours as he walked, but could come
to no understanding of it. And while he was puzzling, he paid slight attention to where he was
going. Soon he left the small deer trail he had
been following and somehow found himself pushing through briars and clambering over fallen logs.

It was midway through the day when he realized that he was not only hungry, he was terribly
lost.

Now the woods were dark and filled, unaccountably, with large gullies lined with ash and
spindletree and the spikey gorse leaves. Nettles
seemed to fence in every new path he chose, as

if the woods itself wanted him to go in one direction and one direction only.

By the time he emerged on the other side of one particular ravine, he was soaking wet, part perspiration, part rain, for a fine mist had formed around the ravine's edge, showering down on anything in it. The mist obscured how far he had to climb, how far he had already come.

When he finally crested through the mist, he found himself on a flat piece of land in which grass—such a deep green it looked like an ocean—spread out as far as he could see.

He laughed out loud. If he had been younger, he might have believed he had discovered the land of fairies, for everything seemed jewel-like and perfect. There were blossoms everywhere, as if autumn had been banished from this land and only summer remained. The place was patchworked with pink stitchwort and rosebay willow herb, yellow spikes of agrimony, and blue and purple thistles. Over all was the buzz of summer insects, broad-bodied dragonflies and the long-legged crane fly. He waded through the grass and flowers, the sweet, soft smell almost making him light-headed. Then the sun broke through and everything shimmered as though touched by a magician's wand.

"This ... this ... this ..." he whispered wildly, intoxicated by it all. A cuckoo called out to him and, in his joy, he answered it back.

His voice echoed over and over and, with it, came another sound: the baying of a hound.

Fowler, came his immediate thought, *and his awful dog.* Could they have tracked him so easily and so far?

But then a second and a third hound's voice joined in and he knew the truth of it. There was a pack of wild dogs on his trail and here he was, stuck in the middle of a meadow with no idea in which direction safety lay. Even at eight, he would not have become so beguiled as to forget all danger and stray from the safety of the trees.

He forced himself to remain calm. "Do not," he whispered, "rise to the lure." Turning carefully about, he noted that the closest line of trees lay ahead of him rather than behind. Without another thought, he began to plunge through the high grass toward them.

What had seemed so beautiful and jewel-like moments before now proved stubborn and treacherous. He could make little time through the grass, and the sound of the dogs' bellings seemed closer and closer with each difficult step. But the cries only forced him into greater effort; he swam agonizingly, through the pinks and yellows and purples and blues that topped the green waves.

He was about twenty steps away from the safety of the trees when he heard the dogs close at his heels, no longer baying but snarling. Not being the kind of lad to give up, he kept on running, his breath coming in shorter and shorter gasps, an awful red-hot ache in his chest.

And then something burst through the grass in front of him, something shaggy and hairy and big as a bear. It reached out and grabbed him up, and though he had not the breath to scream, he screamed.

4. CREATURE

THE CREATURE TOOK FIVE STEPS, NO more, and leaped up into an old oak, the boy now snugged under its arm. Behind it, the dogs were snarling and yelping in equal measure, but they were too late. The creature was already into the tree, scrambling upward with such quickness, it reached the third branching of the tree trunk before the pack had ringed the oak below.

All the while the boy kept screaming, a high, horrible sound that he had not known he could make. At each scream, the dogs set up an echoing wail.

The creature set the boy down next to its side and put a shaggy finger over his mouth.

"Hush ye," it said.

And the boy realized all at once that it was not in fact a creature that had rescued him, but a man. An enormous, ugly, hairy, one-eyed man. A wild man, a *wodewose*.

The boy stopped screaming.

The two sat across from one another on the thick branch in silence while below, the dogs—now equally silenced—circled and circled. The boy was still hot and cold with fright; the wild man's ugly, ridged, scarred face with its bulbous nose and one blind eye did nothing to reassure him. But as the wild man made no move to harm him, the boy finally understood that the wode-wose had, for whatever reasons, risked his own life to rescue him. So at last the boy relaxed. He even tried to smile at the wild man. However, the gapped grin he got in return did not help his sense of dis-ease.

The boy stared down at the circling pack and the dogs returned his stare. There were seven dogs in all, the largest a brindled mastiff, the smallest a stubby-legged rathound. None looked particularly well fed, and the ones with the heavy coats were matted with burrs. He could not tell which one was the leader of the pack, though he guessed it to be the mastiff by its size. He was startled by the liquid shine of their eyes.

Dogs, his conscious mind told him. But as he continued to gaze down, he became mesmerized by them, and suddenly he found himself shoulder to shoulder, nose to nose with the dogs under the shadowy canopy of leaves.

Now he understood it was *not* the mastiff who led the pack, for while it had the mass, it was not particularly intelligent. The leader was a smaller, broad-chested bulldog with large, yellowing teeth.

The dogs looked at him quizzically and sniffed him over: nose, neck, legs, rear. He sniffed them back; their familiar rank smell spoke of hunger and fear/not fear. He found to his surprise that he could read each dog by its stink.

The bulldog lifted its leg against the oak, marking the tree, then turned to speak in a high tenor voice. "Take your place."

The others answered in short, sharp agreement. "Place...place...place."

The boy sang along with them, as if he had no ideas of his own, only the single mind of the pack. "Place!" he cried out.

As if pleased with this response, the bulldog turned its back and started off across the green meadow, the others trailing behind. Soon all the boy could see of them was the swath they had cut through the grass. He took one step after them, then another, blinked, and found himself sitting once more in the oak tree, the wild man across from him.

"Place," the boy whispered.

The wodewose shook his head. "Packs got no reason, lad," he said. "Thee must not run with them. Place be what is wrong with the world." Then he leaped from the tree and headed into the deeper woods.

"Wait!" the boy cried out.

But the wild man was gone.

5. WILD FOLK

HE FOLLOWED THE WODEWOSE FOR SEV-eral hours, stopping only to gather late bramble-berries to quiet the rumbling of his stomach. It was not until nearly the very end of his journey that he understood that the wild man had left him a readable trail on purpose: a broken branch here, a bit of fur caught on briar there, a scuffed foot-print. As long as he looked carefully, there were signs.

He had no doubt the wild man could have gone through the woods leaving no sign at all. He had heard the stories. How the wodewose lived in the company of serpents and wolves and the mammoth forest bulls. How their strength lay in their shaggy locks which if shorn left them pitiful and weak. How they lived on water and flesh, the water from the streams and the raw flesh of wild beasts. How like kings in their castles, they ruled a great domain, but their vassals were stag and doe, boar and sow, he-bear and she-bear, all the inhabitants of the wood.

As he remembered the tales, he lost the thread of the wild man's trail and stumbled—as if by chance—into another meadow that was small and manageable and ringed by tall beech trees. And there, in tented dwellings, like the Hebrews of old, was an entire town of wild men. And wild women. And wild children as well.

Astonished, he stood for a moment, unmoving.

It was one of the wild children who first spotted him, calling out in a high, thin voice, the accent almost masking meaning, "Look, 'ee, wha' cum 'ere."

Alerted, the rest of the wild folk looked up from their chores. Some had been stretching hides, some cutting great logs, still others turning spitted meat over small cookfires. But at the child's warning—for warning it seemed to be—they stared at the intruder and cried out as with a single voice some kind of wild ululation.

Slowly, hands out to show he meant them no harm, the boy came into their midst and they all arose, ringing him round. The men were in the front, women and children behind.

He tried not to stare at them but could not help himself. They were to a man shaggy, dressed in leather skins and jackets of fur, with unkempt beards and long, straggly locks; their faces were all horribly scarred and scored as if with fire or brands. The women were more civilized looking, their hair less matted, many carefully braided. The skin clothing the women wore was decorated with feathers and quills. One woman, with bright red hair, had even plaited flowers in her hair.

The children were indistinguishable boys from girls in their deerskin clothing and unbound locks. He did not think he could tell any of them apart, except that some were more delicately featured and these he took to be girls. He was to discover later on that this was not always true.

"Where...is...the...one...who...found... me?" he asked, spacing his words out carefully and gesturing broadly, as if talking to an infant or to a person from another land. He was not sure if they could understand his dialect.

A babble of voices surrounded him, their language like water over stone. The children laughed, hiding their mouths behind their hands.

"They laugh at the slowness of thy tongue," came a familiar low voice.

The boy turned and saw the one-eyed wodewose.

"The children laugh at thy clothing, never having seen any like it. Thee art a strange sight to them," the wodewose continued.

The soft laughter came again.

"Never?"

"We keep ourselves to ourselves," the wodewose said, and the adults nodded in agreement. "'Tis better that way. We who are grown have seen too much o' the world outside our woods. War and plague and the branding of those who be taking from the overfull larders of the rich to feed their own starving children. The slander of innocents, the burning of witches, the beating of women. We be having enough o' that."

There was a low murmur that ran around the

circle, a dark complement to the light childish laughter.

The boy nodded.

"Best we bring thee food," the wild man said. "Thee hath made long passage to find us." He started to turn. "Come!" he said, looking over his shoulder.

The crowd broke apart to let the boy through and he followed the wodewose, needing two steps to the wild man's one. He could feel the wild folk behind him staring silently. But one small child, whose white-blond shoulder-length hair fairly glowed in the sunlight, followed right at his heels, crying out, "'Oo be thee? 'Uht be thee?" till he turned suddenly and stared down at the child. With a delighted gasp, the child scampered away and hid behind a tent.

"Do not let our Cub affright thee," the wodewose said.

The boy found that funny and he laughed out loud. "I think rather I affrighted the Cub."

"Aught affrights that one," the wodewose said, but with such affection, the boy wondered if the child were the wild man's own. "'Tis all a game for that one. Dogs, wolves, even bears. He comes home with them, one and all. They follow him and do us no harm. He be growing up a king o' these woods."

"Is that possible?" the boy asked, but in a quiet, respectful voice, because suddenly it seemed to him that with these wild folk anything was possible. Anything at all.

6. BEDDING

DINNER WAS LIKE—AND NOT LIKE—DINners the boy had had before. Not only did the wild folk roast spit meat on open fires, but they cooked leeks and wild garlic, mushrooms and dark root vegetables in earthenware vessels buried in the coals. At the end of the meal there was even a pudding of wild plums flavored—so the wodewose told him—with sweet cicely. The boy had not been so full except for dining in Duke Vortigern's kitchen the one time.

"Do you always eat this way?" he asked.

"This way...that way..." Cub said. He sat snugged up 'twixt boy and wodewose.

The wodewose laughed, his good eye closing to

a slit. "In wintertide it be sparer. But we know the woods and we know where the food be. We build no stone houses for we must go where needs send. But all the forest be our place." He cuffed Cub good-naturedly; the child giggled at the soft blow and settled under the man's arm.

"Does he stay then?" asked one of the women, pointing to the boy. She had bristly black hair and something like a brand on her cheek.

A second woman, the redhead, added, "Thems that eats, works."

The women set up a babble of agreement until the wild man held up his hand. They silenced at once.

"He be abandoned in the woods," the wode-wose said. "He be one of ours."

The black-haired woman spat to one side. "He be too old for abandoning. Like as not he's run off."

"Run away or thrown away," the wodewose said, "he be ours. Can thee honestly say *thee* did not run off?"

The dark-haired woman gave the wodewose an unreadable look and walked away. After a moment, the other women followed her.

The boy was uneasy with what he had just heard. "I do not mean to stay with you more than this one night," he said. "I do not intend to be a…"

"A wild man?" The wodewose laughed, but this time his eye did not become a slit. "Art thee not one already?"

The boy did not answer. He had meant to say he did not intend to be a trouble to them. He feared that his trail might yet lead Fowler to this quiet camp. And if Fowler, why not Vortigern and his men? But the wodewose's question bothered him so much, he knew he would have to give it thought. Once he had, indeed, lived in the woods on his own, thrown away by someone whose face he had never been able to recall, not even in dreams. But this time he was in the woods because he had willed it himself. Was there a difference? And if there was, what should be his response to it?

"Come," the wodewose said, breaking through the boy's reverie. "I will show thee where to sleep the night."

They walked to one of the hide tents and the

wild man gestured to it. "This be the tent for boys. Till thee has a name."

"But I already have a name," the boy said. "Two actually. Hawk. And Hobby." He did not give his true name, Merlin, which was another kind of hawk altogether. For some reason, it suddenly seemed important to him to keep that name hidden.

"Woods name be one thing, town name an other," said the wodewose.

The boy nodded. He had always known names were powerful, so it did not surprise him that the wild man knew it, too.

"Now, Hawk-Hobby, thee must make thy own bed. No one serves an other here. No one rules an other here. As the Greenwitch says, if thee eats with us, thee must work with us."

"What do I make the bed of?" Hawk-Hobby asked. When he had lived in the woods before, he had had no regular bed but had lain in trees for safety, a different tree each night. When he had lived at Master Robin's farm, Mag and Nell had stuffed his mattress with dried grasses and his comforter with feathers from the geese. When he had traveled with the players Ambrosius and Viviane, he had slept in a box bed in their cart. He had actually never made a bed for himself.

"Thy place, thy choice," the wodewose said, holding up the tent flap for the boy to enter. "So thee must choose with care." Then he dropped the flap and was gone.

Looking around the tent, the boy saw there were already several beds—hide pallets actually —but they were clearly spoken for. The imprint of bodies was on them and there were yew bows and arrows by the side of two of the beds, a stick dolly by another. He went over to one of the hides and put his hand inside, drawing out a bit of the bedding. It consisted of dried grasses and was musty smelling; not at all sweet, like Mag's stuffing.

The wodewose was gone and there was no one in the tent to ask, so he lifted up the flap and looked about the camp. There seemed to be only women working for the moment, and frankly they all frightened him.

"I will find something by myself," he murmured. The grass around the camp was all trampled down, and he knew he would prefer something fresh. So he walked to the meadow's edge, listening carefully for a minute in case he should hear again the baying of hounds. Then he plunged into the woods.

There was something resembling a trail and he followed it, noting his surroundings carefully so he did not get lost. Light was still plentiful in the meadow, but the trail through the woods was already grey with the coming night. Fifteen minutes from the camp he came upon another patch of high meadow and, near it, a tangle of flowering marjoram. He had no carry-bag, so he stripped off his shirt, bundling the grasses and spicy herb together.

Never minding that his chest and arms were now goosefleshed with the cold, he hoisted the full shirt-bag and followed the path back to the camp. He was sure the women would be pleased with his energy.

No one paid him any mind when he returned. So he found the boys' tent and went in. When he had dumped his precious grasses into an empty hide mattress, the thing was not even a quarter full.

He had to make five trips in all before he had

the bed full enough to sleep on. By then it was dark, and he was so exhausted he could have slept on the ground. No other boys were yet in the tent, but he was too tired to care. He lay down and fell into a sleep as soft as the bed. His dreams—whatever they were—were as spicy as the herb.

7. QUARRELS

HAWK-HOBBY WOKE TO A LOUD NOISE OUT-
side the tent. For a moment he feared that Fowler
had found the camp, then realized the voices
were all women's. And they were quarreling.

He sat up, leaning on one elbow, and saw that
the other beds in the tent were now occupied by
five boys near his age, and on another the child,
Cub, was curled around the stick dolly. The boys
were all laughing silently, hands across their
mouths.

"What does it mean?" Hawk-Hobby asked,
pointing toward the sound of the women's argument.

"'Ee..." one boy said, his hand barely moving

from his mouth. Then he was convulsed again with silent laughter, and falling back on his bed.

"'Ee..." a second boy added. "They mock 'ee." He, too, collapsed backward with a fit of giggles.

The other boys did not even try to speak, so caught were they by the joke's contagion.

Cub did not laugh. He got off his pallet and came over to Hawk-Hobby, handing him the stick dolly. "Poppet will guard 'ee from the women," he said with great seriousness. Then he went over to the tent flap and lifted it slightly to listen. After a moment, he turned back, "Ooooo, what has 'ee done?"

"I have done nothing," Hawk-Hobby said, suddenly consumed by guilt for all that he actually had done long before he met the wild folk. He stood up and went over to the tent flap to listen. But when he stuck his head out, the women saw him and their indignation rose even louder till the wodewose himself left the cookfire where the men were huddled.

"Na, na," he said, by way of trying to quiet the women. It was only when he held up his hands in mock surrender that they were finally still.

"Come out, boy," he called to Hawk-Hobby.

Hawk-Hobby started out, remembered the stick dolly, and gave it back to the child. "Best keep Poppet from this trouble, whatever it be," he said. He meant it half humorously, but Cub took the dolly and scrambled back onto his bed to store the stick doll there.

"What ails them?" Hawk-Hobby asked, with a lightness he certainly did not feel.

"They be angry with thee," the wodewose said. "It never be wise to anger women."

"But what have I done?" asked Hawk-Hobby. "I have done nothing wrong."

"Wrongness be in the beholder's eye," the wodewose said. "Else we all be innocents indeed." He smiled, but it was not reassuring. "Bring out thy bedding. I cannot go in, for I be a man and that be the boys' tent."

Puzzled, Hawk-Hobby went back and dragged out his bedding, grimly aware that the boys were still laughing at him. But little Cub, at least, tried to help, holding up one end of the hide. That he proved more trouble than help did not matter. Hawk-Hobby gave him a wink by way of thanks and Cub's face immediately lit up.

No sooner was the mattress clear of the tent

flap than the women circled it and began pulling the bedding apart, roughly grabbing out handsful of grass and spreading them on the ground.

"Here, I worked..." Hawk-Hobby began, but was silenced when the black-haired woman with the scar held up some sprigs of grey-tinted marjoram leaves, now almost black.

"Organy!" she cried in triumph, and the women with her set up caterwauling anew and tore apart the rest of his bedding.

"Organy," breathed Cub next to him. "Oooo, that be bad indeed."

The wodewose grabbed Hawk-Hobby by the arm and led him around the side of the tent, away from the angry women. Cub trotted at their heels. "Thy bed," the wodewose said wearily, "be stuffed with a particular herb. *Organy* in the old tongue. It has many virtues: it cures bitings and stingings of venom, it be proof against stuffed lungs or the swounding of the heart. But it never be used for bedding as it be too precious for that."

"I...I did not know," Hawk-Hobby said miserably.

"'Ee did not know," echoed Cub. "'Ee *did* not."

"Hush ye," said the wodewose, "and be about

thy own business." He raised his hand and Cub scampered away around the tent, though Hawk-Hobby could see by the child's shadow that he stopped at the corner and was still listening.

"I only wanted it for the sweet smell," Hawk-Hobby explained. Indeed, it was the truth.

"For the sweet smell?" Clearly the wild man was puzzled.

"Sweet herbs for sweet dreams," Hawk-Hobby finished lamely.

"Dreams!" Cub came skipping back around the corner of the tent. "'Ee has dreams. We like dreams."

"I said to be about thy own business, young Cub. Dreams be not the provenance of children." The wodewose's face was dark, as if a shadow had come over it. He turned back to Hawk-Hobby. "Does thee dream?"

"Does not everybody dream?" Hawk-Hobby was reluctant to discuss his magic with the wild man. But—as if a geas, a binding spell, had been laid upon him—he had to answer when asked about it. And answer truthfully. Though he could give those answers aslant.

"There be night dreams...and others," the wild

man said. "And I saw thee dream with the dogs yester morn. Why else would I blaze thee a trail here? Still, I be not certain..."

Hawk-Hobby waited. There was nothing to be answered.

"Be thee...a dream-reader?" the wodewose asked carefully.

Just as carefully, Hawk-Hobby replied. "I have been called so."

"And be thee called in truth?"

Hawk-Hobby sighed. There was no getting by that question. "I surely know what my dreams mean. Or at least I often do." It had seemed at first such a small magic, but everyone was so interested in it. It *had* to mean more.

"Ahhh," the wodewose said. Then he turned abruptly and walked around the tent, calling out to the women in his rumble of a voice: "He be a dream-reader. And we without since the last old one died."

"'Ee surely needs Poppet now," said Cub. "I will bring it to 'ee." He disappeared into the tent.

No sooner was the child gone than the women rounded the corner, arguing as they came.

"He be too young," said the redhead.

"Let him prove it," said an older woman, her hair greying at the temples.

"But why would he say..." the wodewose began. But the women would not let him finish. They grabbed up Hawk-Hobby by the arm, three on one side, three on the other, two behind him. They dragged him back to the mattress, now nothing but a flattened hide, and thrust him down.

"Dream," the black-haired woman commanded.

"Dream," they all cried as if with one voice.

"What? Here? Now?"

Their stone faces were his only answers, so he closed his eyes and called for a dream. Any dream.

Of course no dream came.

8. THE LONG WAIT

THEY KEPT HIM ON THE HIDE FOR HOURS, taking turns watching him. It was a warm autumn day and the sun was blazing in an unclouded sky. Whenever he attempted to leave the hide—to get out of the sun or to relieve himself or simply to stand and stretch—the women made menacing noises and threatened him with long sticks. Then he recalled the stories he had heard about the wild women, stories Mag and Nell had told him when he had been a boy in Master Robin's house: how the wild women stole away human children and ate them.

For the first time he was really afraid.

So he tried once again to dream. Closing his

eyes, he thought about pleasanter times with Master Robin or the happy days in Ambrosius' cart. But the more he tried to dream, the wider awake he remained.

The women did not speak to him, nor with one another, while they were on guard. Their aptitude for silence was appalling.

Very well, he thought. *I will match you in this long wait. I will outlast you.* It occurred to him that as long as they waited for him to dream, they would not be eating him.

Opening his eyes, he stared at each woman in turn. Two he was already familiar with: the branded woman and the redhead. They seemed to be the leaders. But soon he found he could distinguish the others as well. In the tales, the wild women were ugly. Mag had said they were covered with bristles and Nell that their black hair was spotted with moss and lichen. But in fact several of the women of this camp were flaxen-haired and none, as far as he could tell, had bristles. As for being ugly, two or three of them were surprisingly good-looking. And the red-head—though she had a tendency to scowl at him, which wrinkled her forehead—was quite beautiful. *Not,* he reminded himself, *as beautiful as Viviane, the lady of the green castle-cart. But close.*

Neither his staring nor his silence seemed to bother the women. Theirs was a genius for long patience. So after a while, Hawk-Hobby forced himself to look down at the ground to avoid their accusing eyes.

Organy, he thought. Even the smell of it would ever after remind him of their stares and the sun beating down on his uncovered head.

On the ground there were hundreds of ants scurrying between the blades of grass. He was startled by their purposefulness in the midst of his own forced idleness.

Ants, his conscious mind told him. But as he continued staring at the hurrying insects, he became mesmerized by them and suddenly he found himself head to abdomen with them as they threaded their way between towering grasses.

The ants were all yellowish-brown and their elbowed feelers swayed before them to a rhythm he could almost grasp. The sound of the many pairs of marching feet was thunderous. Plodding through the arcade of grass, they marched as if a single thread connected them. They sang as one: "Go the track, don't look back. Go the track. Don't look back." The words repeated over and over. It was hypnotic.

He opened his mouth to sing with them, blinked, and found himself once more sitting on the hide. But the song of the ants was still so compelling, he found himself singing it. "Go the track. Don't look back."

He was interrupted by the women crying out: "The Dreamer. The Dreamer is here."

"But..." he tried to say, "that was no dream." However, he did not know *what* it was, so he forced himself to silence. If the women thought him this Dreamer, and that got him off the hide, allowed him to stretch his legs, or relieve himself, he would agree to anything.

He thought he had been on the hide for hours and hours but when he looked up at the sun, it was not quite noon.

9. DREAMER

THEY FED HIM THEN, EVEN MORE THAN they had at dinner, a strange porridge and a stew that left an odd aftertaste. They made him eat every bite.

He ate steadily and then, when he thought he could not eat anything more, they brought him a sweet honey drink which they insisted he finish. He tried to turn it down but they would not let him. To silence them, he drank it all. At last, with aching, taut belly, he tried to stand and found his legs would not hold him up.

"I feel…" he began, not knowing what he was feeling. And turning his head to one side, he was suddenly and quite efficiently sick.

When he was done, the women helped him stand and guided him to a place somewhere on the edge of the camp. Through slotted eyes he tried to make it out, but could not. His head was swimming about and he was afraid he might be sick again.

"This be thy place now," the black-haired woman with the cheek brand was saying, her voice remarkably similar to the bulldog's.

Place. That was good, he thought drowsily. He needed a place.

The woman gave him a little push in the small of his back and he fell, rather than walked, into it.

The place was small and dark and closely covered. There was some sort of mattress, thin and old smelling. He did not care. He curled up on it and fell instantly to sleep.

This time he dreamed.

He dreamed of the bear again, but now he was in the dream as well, holding a sword in one hand, a large stone in the other. The bear took off its crown and flung it onto the sword. At that, sword and crown dissolved and he woke sweating and ill.

It did not help that his small, closed-in tent seemed to be swaying. It did not help that the air stank of his sickness. He tried to get to his feet and banged his shoulder painfully against something. His head hurt. His belly ached. The slightest noise hammered at his temples like a blacksmith's hammer on an anvil.

Heavily he fell again onto his pallet where he slept, dreamed, woke, slept again. The dream images all blended into one great dream of kings and kingdoms.

Suddenly an enormous light—like the light of heaven itself—flooded into his dream. He opened his eyes and found that he was lying in an open space. The tent had been lifted away and the light was the new day.

Only then did he see what his *place* really was. He was in some sort of large wicker cage hanging from a tree limb some five feet off the ground. When he tried the cage door, it would not open. Not that this was exactly a surprise. It was tied shut with a complicated knot on the outside that he could not reach, no matter how hard he tried.

A cage. Like a criminal hung up at the crossroads to starve. Or like the sacrifice of the Druid priests.

"Or like," he whispered to himself, "a beast in a trap." He thought wildly: *They are fattening me for a feast.*

He gazed about. He seemed to be alone. Once more he tried to reach the knot, straining his arm as far as it could go. He could touch it...but just. There was no way he could get it untied. *What a fool I have been,* he thought. *Stuffing myself when I should have been starving.* He sat back down heavily on the pallet. The movement caused the cage to sway and his stomach to heave.

"Dreamer!" A woman's voice called and reluctantly he looked toward the sound. It was the red-headed woman. How could he ever have thought such a witch beautiful? "Dreamer!" Her voice made his head ache the more. "Here be herbs for thy sickness. For thy stomach, cuckoo's meat; it will strengthen thy belly and procure thy appetite. And this other..." she pointed to a smaller vessel, "bruisewort. That thee must sniff up into thy nostrils and it will purge thy head. We apologize for the ruse. But it be necessary to take thee, unprotesting, to thy place."

"Go away, witch," he mumbled. His own voice hurt his head as well.

"Once thy sickness be gone, we will hear thy dreams."

"I will take nothing from your hands. Nothing. I will starve myself before I take something from you. Then what kind of a meal will I make?" It was, he thought, a strong speech. That was why he was stunned when she began to laugh. It was a pretty laugh, soft, tinkling.

"Eat thee? Eat another human soul? What does thee take us for?"

Was this a trick? He could not think, his head hurt so.

"All we want from thee are thy dreams. Come, take these herbals. They will cure what ails thee." She held out the vessels again.

He did not have the will to argue longer. *And,* he reminded himself, *to escape he would need a clear head.*

"Give them here," he said, and she put the vessels into his hand. He took the stuff as ordered, drinking the one, sniffing the other, which made him sneeze five times in a row. The sneezing did not help his hurting head.

But within the hour, almost miraculously, he felt quite bright-headed, and his stomach no longer ached. This time when he looked out from the cage, the scene below him took on a serene beauty. The wild men were stretching hide skins between saplings; the women, in a cluster, pushed bone needles through deerskin, gossiping happily. Throughout the camp the children played games that he recognized: beggar-thy-neighbor, leap-frogs, hide-then-seek, and tag.

It looked like any country village. Like a home.

Except...he thought...except their houses were tents, there were no streets, and he was stuck up in a wicker cage, suspended in the air, while his captors were waited for him to read his dreams.

What else they might want of him, should his dreaming fail, he was too afraid to ask.

10. DREAM CAGE

HE HAD NO IDEA HOW MANY DAYS HE RE-
mained in the cage. He tried to keep them separate in his mind, but they tended to run together.
Each time he woke, the women gave him an
herbal draught, then listened to his latest dreams.
He never lied about the dreams, nor made one
up. Indeed, he could not have, even had he
wanted to.

He dreamed of a table round as a wheel that
rolled across the land leaving great wide ruts. He
dreamed of huge stones walking across the ocean.
He dreamed of a giant, green as May, who threw
his head in the air like a child with a ball. He
dreamed of a man and a woman asleep in one

bed, a sword between them sharper than any desire.

He told the wild women all these dreams.

At each telling, they listened politely, then debated among themselves the meanings of the dreams. The table, they said, was the year, sometimes winter and sometimes summer. The stones, they said, were the Saxon army come across the sea. The giant, they said, was the Green Man come to save them. The man and woman and sword, they said, were of no consequence, having naught to do with them, but with the nobles in their fancy houses.

They never asked him what he thought of the dreams, and here they erred. For they were mistaken in every particular about the dreams, this he knew. The dreams were each a slantwise reading of his own future. He was sure of it. They had nothing to do with the wild folk at all.

None of the men or children came near the cage. Dreaming, it seemed, was the provenance of women. None, that is, but the child Cub, who stood back a ways to be able to see into the cage, but did not speak. It was not that the child was shy, lest he had been made shy by Hawk-Hobby's elevation to Dreamer. But the distance he had to stand made conversation awkward. He was only a small child, after all.

One morning—perhaps it was the third or fourth—desperate for information or even a more human encounter, Hawk-Hobby called out to the child: "How is that Poppet of yours?"

Cub opened his mouth to answer, thought better of it, and scampered away. But he appeared again soon after with the dolly in hand. Throwing it with careful aim up into the cage, he cried out, "Poppet will guard 'ee." Then he ran off again and this time did not come back.

"Poppet didn't do such a good job last time," Hawk-Hobby mused, but he kept the doll, tucked up under his pallet. Indeed, the child did not come close again so he could not return the toy.

A day or so later, when he had been taken from the cage by the women to cleanse himself in a nearby stream, he suddenly realized why he had had trouble counting off the days in the cage.

"They have put something in my food," he whispered to himself. "Something to make me sleep.

Something to encourage me to dream." The sound of the river hid his words from the wild women guarding him on the shore.

He wondered that it had taken him so long to figure it out, then guessed that the draughts themselves had kept him from the knowledge. He realized, too, that *anyone* so drugged would dream. "Which is why," he whispered, "the wild folk would ordinarily only use the old ones, the ones past hunting or harvesting. The old ones whose bones are too brittle to carry them through the woods. It would be a mercy, really, for them to be so employed; a mercy to dream away the tag ends of their lives." He remembered how surprised they had been that he admitted to being a dreamer.

But, he thought, *I am a dreamer even without the draughts.* And for the first time he wondered —really wondered—what good this dreaming was to him. As a warning, a dream was all but useless if it could not be properly read. How was he to learn, beyond his instinctive guesses, the language of his dreams? Who was he to tell what he discovered therein? Such dreams might guide kings and kingdoms. Such dreams might prophesy the movements of armies. Such dreams might direct the marriage of princes, the death of queens, and the birth of royal babes. But what good were they here in the wild amongst the wodewose?

"And what good are they," he said to himself, "in the hands of a boy like me?"

He was still puzzling it out when they returned him to the wicker cage. He refused to eat or drink. "I do not need this to dream," he told them.

They did not believe him. But they no longer had the power to compel.

They brought him food in the small clay bowls and he refused it all. For two days he was the captive of bad dreams.

He slept curled over an aching belly, Poppet clutched in his arms. He woke sweating and hollow. He shook. He shivered. His bones felt like fire, then ice. Many times he was on the verge of crying out for one of the draughts. But Poppet would caution him in Cub's voice. "Do not rise to the lure," the dolly said. "This is *not* your place. Go the track. Don't look back." In his true waking moments he knew that Poppet did not talk. But deep in his dreams he was not so sure.

"Dreamer," other voices, women's voices, cozzened him. "Eat. Drink. This will cure what ails thee." But he continued to resist, saying, "I do not need that to dream. I do not need that to dream."

The women did not believe him, of course, but they watched as his body cleansed itself of all their herbs. And when he finally sat up without shaking, the only one to see him was Cub, who watched silent and still.

"Here," Hawk-Hobby called to the child. "Take Poppet. It has guarded me well. Now it must guard you."

The child shook his head, but came over anyway and Hawk-Hobby held the doll out to him.

The moment Cub's hand touched the dolly, something odd and wild and strange seemed to bond them. It was as if a spark of lightning shot from one hand, through the poppet, to the other.

And Hawk-Hobby dreamed.

He dreamed that in the meadow a fountain of blood burst through the grass. It covered the feet of the wild folk, rose to their ankles, kept rising till it covered their shoulders, necks, heads. They cried out for help, but there was no sound. And Poppet alone escaped, sailing over the river of blood in the wicker cage, the sails powered by its own breath.

It was his first dream about the wild folk themselves.

And his last.

11. MAGIC

IT WAS AN AWFUL DREAM. TERRIBLE. HE woke from it screaming.

Cub grabbed Poppet and stumbled back from the force of the scream, then turned and ran screaming himself into the midst of the women.

Hawk-Hobby could not hear what the child said. He was too far away for that. But clearly whatever Cub said startled the women, shocking them into action. They all came toward the cage at a run, and the men—a bit more tentatively—behind them.

"What was thy dream, Dreamer?" the black-haired woman asked.

He told it all: the meadow, the blood, the doll, the boat, the breath.

There was much consternation among them as they discussed the dream. Though they did not ask him what it meant, much they could read on their own. The meadow filled with blood was too obvious to ignore. Arguments over, they turned as one to begin the work of packing up the camp.

"Ask me," he called after them. He thought he knew more than they had found in the dream. He was, himself, the doll; a toy in the wrong hands, a magic creature in the right. With his breath he could work magic. Magic more powerful than the spilling of blood. Surely *that* is what the dream meant. But someone needed to ask before he could answer. He understood that much about his ability to read dreams.

It was as though they had forgotten him completely. They were much too busy with their move. Striking the tents, the men rolled them into tight bundles. The women covered the campfires with dirt, then sorted through the drying herbs and strips of meat. Even the children worked, placing clothes and other small belongings into packs. If they all seemed to agree on one thing, it was that the meadow was a place of coming destruction. Blood. They were best gone from it. And quickly.

Only Cub was oblivious to the activity, intent, instead, on something on the ground.

From so far away Hawk-Hobby could not see what fascinated the child. But when a woman, noticing the idle child, cuffed him roughly, both Cub and Hawk-Hobby cried out at the same time: Cub because his ear rang with the blow and the caged Dreamer because his own ear ached in sympathy, as if he and the child were now one.

Cub turned slowly at the sound of the Dreamer's voice, his hand still cupped over his aching ear. Then his face lit up and he bent down to pick up the thing from the ground. Running over, he smiled up at Hawk-Hobby. There were streaks on his cheeks where tears had run down but he was no longer crying.

"Look!" he said, holding up a grubby hand. There was a robin in his open palm, its head hanging to one side as if its neck were broken. "Make robin sing, Dreamer. Make robin fly."

Hawk-Hobby took the bird without hesitation, not quite knowing why. The child's request was gentle enough. More a plea than a demand. But for some reason it seemed as strong as a geas, a magic compulsion. He took the bird and looked down at it. Its orange breast was already dulled in death and there was not so much as a murmur beneath its feathers. Its eyes were cloudy and its little feet stiff.

"'Ee must fix it, Dreamer," the child said.

"And you must get me Poppet. To guard the bird," Hawk-Hobby said. He said it more to gain time than because he thought it might be any help.

The child ran off to fetch his dolly. Hawk-Hobby sat down in the cage, his legs swinging over the side. He remembered the magician Ambrosius bringing flowers out of his sleeves and coins from behind a man's ear. Such magicks, he had soon found out, were but sleights of hand. One needed to have flowers up one's sleeve to bring them down. One needed a coin hid in the palm to make it appear at a man's ear. What the child was asking of him was more than that, was the very breath of life.

Breath.

That was one component of the dream. The

poppet's breath powering the sails of the wicker boat.

He brought the little bird up even with his face. Close it was even more pathetic, already cooling. Parting its beak with two careful fingers and then closing his eyes, he remembered the exact feeling in the dream and blew three short breaths into the bird. They were small breaths—of air, of life. He did not know what else to do.

For a long moment nothing happened. Nothing at all. Except that the clearing and the woods stilled around him.

Then, as if a light had come down from heaven, piercing his head, and a second light had come up from earth, through his feet, he was shot through with a great energy. Between his palms the bird began to warm. A small flutter started beneath the flame-colored breast. The legs twitched, so hard one of the tiny nails on its feet scratched his finger.

"Tic!" the bird said suddenly, sharply. "Tic!" Then it poured out the clear jangling warble of its autumn song.

Stunned—but not really surprised—Hawk-Hobby threw the bird into the open air where it shook its wings and, still singing, flew off into the sky.

Exhausted by his first real magic, Hawk-Hobby sank back onto the hide pallet, suddenly too tired to do more.

12. FREEDOM

TWO PEOPLE—AND TWO ONLY—HAD SEEN what happened. Cub had crept back, dolly in hand, and watched as the robin lifted off the boy's sweaty palm and flung itself into the lightening air. The other watcher was the wodewose himself, standing to one side, his good eye blinking as if not quite crediting what he had seen.

"Surely," the man said to himself, "thee be much more than a dreamer." He left the hide he had been packing and strode over to the cage.

"Who art thee?" he demanded. "What art thee?"

"He is Dreamer," the child said, satisfied. "He is Breath of Dream. He is Maker."

The wodewose paid the child no attention. "What art thee?" he asked again.

"I am a boy," Hawk-Hobby answered carefully, but the magic demanded more of him now. A direct answer to a direct question. "I am…" And suddenly he realized he did not know *what* he was any longer. Boy. Man. Mage. In one brilliant light-filled moment he had been changed beyond all recognition.

What am I indeed? he wondered. *A magician full of tricks and misdirections like Ambrosius? Or a wizard in truth?* He had made a dead bird fly. *Perhaps*…he thought recklessly, *perhaps I am a god. Or a demon.* Vaguely he recalled, as if it had been a dream, someone calling him that. *What am I indeed?*

"I am…an orphan," he said at last. That much he was sure of. "I am alone."

"We take orphans," the wodewose said. "They be our children."

"Take?"

"From hillsides where they be abandoned. From villages where they be abused. From cradles where they be forgotten." There was a kind of mercy in his one good eye. As he spoke his ugly face took on a rough beauty. "We only take what is not wanted."

"As you took me," Hawk-Hobby pointed out. "From the dogs."

The eye suddenly turned crafty. "But did thee run *from* the dogs, or did thee run *with* them?"

Remembering for a moment how he *had* been part of the pack, Hawk-Hobby was silent.

"What art thee?" the wodewose asked again. "Be thee Green Man? Be thee Robin o' the Wood? What hath thee been called?"

"I have been called many things," the boy answered honestly. "I told you that before. I have been called Hawk. I have been called Hobby." He took a breath, remembering the falconer who had found him in the woods and became his first father. Master Robin. He saw suddenly how he could honor the man and remain truthful. "Robin is as good a name as any."

"Hah!" the wodewose exclaimed. "Thee made the robin live again, so thee may be Robin indeed. Be thee merciful to us, Robin." He made a sketchy bob with his head, then his eye suddenly scrunched up. "But Robin o' the Woods is a tricksy spirit. I must think more on this." So saying, he left, walking out into the meadow and leaving the others to their mundane tasks.

But Cub stayed behind. "Be 'ee Robin indeed?" he asked, his eyes wide.

"What is a name," Hawk-Hobby asked, "but the outward dressing of a man?"

"The Green Man must not be caged," the child said. "Robin belongs to all the woods."

"Then open the knot, and let me free."

"I cannot reach it," the child said.

"Get me a knife."

"I have none."

It was an impasse and Hawk-Hobby could not think what to do next, but the child had his own ideas.

"If 'ee be Robin indeed, knots cannot bind 'ee."

"Oh, Cub..." Hawk-Hobby began, his voice sounding a hopeless note. But then he thought, *Why not? How much more difficult was it to make a bird fly?* "Hand me your poppet."

With a sudden rush of courage, the child handed up the dolly, as if expecting to receive another shock and prepared to accept it. But this time there was none.

Hawk-Hobby took the doll and stared at it. Then he held it between his palms and breathed three careful breaths onto its berryjuice mouth. Was it his imagination, or did the stick figure move, ever so slightly, in his hands? He stretched full down on the cage bottom and stuck his hand—with the dolly—as far out of the cage as he could. "Is Poppet near the knot?" he called.

"Down more. And more. There!" The child's voice was full of awe.

"All right, Poppet," Hawk-Hobby said, "do thy will." He held onto the head of the doll and with its stick legs poked at the knot. He could not tell if the dolly moved of its own or if his own manipulations did the work, but suddenly Cub cried out, "There! 'Ee's got it!" and the knot came undone.

The child danced up and down, clapping his hand. "Oh, Green Man, 'ee be free. Free."

He did not take time to argue, but swung the door to the cage wide. It was but a quick jump to the ground and but ten steps to the line of trees. He could hear the women's cries behind him and Cub's singular squawl: "Robin, wait for me!"

But he waited for no one as he ran, ever faster, into the woods.

13. HIDING PLACE

HAWK-HOBBY MADE A PATH WHERE NO
path had been, dodging through the undergrowth
as if the Gabriel hounds, the dogs of hell, were
on his trail. And indeed, the women's ululations
sounded like the baying of a pack.

But at last he tired of running and made the
assumption that no one was following because he
no longer could hear the voices, except as a thin
honking. Looking up to discover the hour through
the trees, he saw a vee of geese heading south,
and laughed. Hounds, women, geese—they all
sounded the same. Mostly, he told himself, he
had been running from his own fear.

He turned to his right and all but fell out onto

235

a track. It was not a thin path such as a deer and its mate might make, nor the higher broken branches of a bear. It was a true road through the woods, the kind a marching army might take.

He shuddered, remembering his dream, then heard a thrashing and crashing behind him. As startled as any wild thing, he glanced back over his shoulder and prepared himself for a second flight.

"Ro...bin..." came the breathy little voice.

"Oh, Cub, you should have stayed with your family," Hawk-Hobby said, and he went to where the child was struggling through the brush. Picking him up he swung the child onto his shoulders.

"'Ee be my family," the child said. "I have taken 'ee as my own."

"You cannot take me..." Hawk-Hobby began, but the child interrupted.

"Silly Robin. Of course I can. We take who is abandoned. We take what is alone. 'Ee said thou wert alone. I take 'ee."

Hawk-Hobby reached up and set the child back down on the ground. He knelt so they were face to face. "They will worry about you. I must bring you back."

"They will put 'ee in the cage again," Cub said.

Hawk-Hobby shrugged. He would have to deal with that after. But first...

"Hush," the child said. "Listen."

But he had already heard. This time it was the baying of hounds in truth as well as the breathy intake of horses. Somewhere up ahead on the track there was a troop on its way. Neither he nor the child believed it was the wild folk.

"What do we do, Robin?" Cub whispered, slipping his hand with the dolly into Hawk-Hobby's. "Will they take us? Will they hurt us?"

"We dare not run, for the dogs will follow and catch us. We must hide."

They faded back into the undergrowth and searched until they found a sturdy oak well away from the path. Hawk-Hobby boosted the child up into the tree crotch then scrambled up quickly behind him. Then alternately pushing and pulling, he got Cub up into the highest branches where they could lie hidden behind the yellowing leaves.

"Pull your legs to your chest like this," he whispered to the child. "Make yourself small. Make yourself invisible."

The child nodded and did as he was instructed.

They lay still but Hawk-Hobby could see that the branch on which the child huddled trembled. *Magic,* he thought frantically. *Now is when I could really use it.* By this he did not mean the breath of life, the moving poppet, the dreams. What good were they to him in this peril? If he could only call down lightning or call up demons or...

And as he was thinking this, a host of horsemen trotted into view. From the treetop he could catch glimpses of them as they rode, two abreast, their armor dusted with the miles. He could see they wore white plumes and had white dragons embossed on their banners and that told him at once who they were: the soldiers he had dreamed of back in the days when he had lived in the green cart. They were the soldiers he had warned Duke Vortigern against. But Duke Vortigern had not believed him, had thrown him out of the castle, out of the town. Hawk-Hobby took some satisfaction in being right.

But only for a moment.

Duke Vortigern had not believed him. But Fowler had. *Fowler!* No sooner had he thought the name than—as if by magic conjuration—the man himself appeared, walking by the side of the horsemen, his massive dog Ranger held fast on a lead.

"I be frightened, Robin," the child whispered.

Hawk-Hobby put a finger to his mouth to shush the boy. "Be like a deer," he whispered back. "Disappear into stillness."

Cub seemed to understand and, like a fawn in danger, he drew back into the tree and all but vanished.

But the dog had caught the sound or their scent. He sniffed the air, gave tentative tongue.

"Hush, dog," Fowler cried out, but he looked where the dog looked. Then he pointed.

The soldiers halted and the man at the lead turned his horse aside and rode over to Fowler and the dog. "What is it, man? What does that hellhound of yours see?"

The dog pulled his master off the track and into the brush, through nettle and bracken and the brittle brown fern. He circled the oak, barking impatiently.

Fowler stared up into the tree, trying to make

out what the dog was barking at. Shaking his bowstring-colored hair out of his eyes, he peered carefully.

Hawk-Hobby closed his eyes and thought about magic. Thought about it as hard as he could.

The dog suddenly went quiet.

"Well?" called the man on the horse.

Fowler, looking up, saw a shimmer of green behind the yellow leaves, as if some bit of sun had pierced the dark canopy, but nothing more. Whatever had irritated the dog was invisible to the eye. "Nothing, my lord Uther. The dog barks at shadows." He stroked his sparse moustache.

"Then we go on," Lord Uther said. "My men are tired and angry after the battle at Carmar then. That bloody Vortigern burned up with all his possessions. These men fight for so little reward and they sorely miss the spoils they were promised. Shut up that hound of yours and let us be out of this woods. There is dark magic here. Some tricksy Green Man magic. I do not like such conjurations. I do not fight shades."

"Yes, my lord," Fowler said, hauling the dog away.

The horseman spun back to the head of his column of soldiers and they went on. It was nearly dark when the last of them was out of sight.

And darker still when the boy and the child dared to climb down from the tree.

14. BATTLEGROUND

"WHERE DO THEY GO, ROBIN?" THE CHILD asked when they were, at last, on solid ground. He asked—but there was already an uncomfortable certainty in his voice. Cub knew—as Hawk-Hobby guessed—that the track led right back to the wodewose camp.

Hawk-Hobby despaired. They had no way of warning the wild folk. Except, of course, he had warned them already with his dream. He only hoped they had been able to escape in time. An angry, tired army would make quick work of them. Not that he had any love for the wild folk. Except for this yellow-haired child, except for the wodewose himself, they had not been good to him. He wanted to be shed of them but he did not wish them dead. Having recently buried Master Robin, Mag, and Nell, he desired only to be done with death.

"We will go softly, quietly, like a fox, like a wolf, back to the camp," he said.

"I can be a fox," Cub said. "I can be a wolf,"

"I know you can," Hawk-Hobby said. "And we will find everyone well and hale. You will see." He patted the child on the head, thinking to himself that he would see Cub back to his family and make his own escape. Having done it once, he was confident he could do it again. But they were no sooner several steps along the track when there was suddenly thunder, great rolling clanging walls of it, and rain bolted down from the sky.

"Robin, I be afraid." The child clutched his hand tightly and shivered with the wet and cold.

Despite his growing magic, Hawk-Hobby was frightened, too. He was, after all, but twelve years old himself. But he would not let the child see his fear. "Come," he said, "we will not stay out in the storm. Let us shelter in the tree."

"Oh, no, Robin," the child said. "Lightning will hurt us there. We must find a cave."

Hawk-Hobby smiled down at him. "Who knows what beast lives in a cave?"

"Thou art Robin o' the Wood," the child said. "No beast be harming 'ee."

"I have no answer for you that will suffice," Hawk-Hobby said. "We will find a cave." And no sooner had he spoken than—as if by magic—they came upon a cave in a cliffside. It was really more a shelf than a cave, too narrow for a beast's den but wide enough to keep them from the rain. Hawk-Hobby went in first and pulled the child in after. And there, huddled together for warmth, they spent a disquieted night.

The track they followed back to the camp had been well widened by the army. Great swaths of bracken had been crushed beneath the horses' hooves; autumn wildflowers had been ground into the dirt.

The child seemed undismayed by the destruction, set as he was on getting to the camp. But at each step, Hawk-Hobby grew colder and colder. It was not fear he was feeling, but dread. It trickled down like sweat between his shoulder blades.

The child stopped suddenly. "Robin. Listen."

Hawk-Hobby listened. He could hear nothing. And then—as if in another dream—he realized: he could hear *nothing*. No birds, no chirruping insects, not even the grunt and moan of trees as they shifted in their roots. *Nothing*.

"Nothing," he said.

"Robin...I want..." and then Cub began to wail, a sound so alien in the woods that it sent a terrible shiver down Hawk-Hobby's spine.

He gathered the child up in his arms and soothed him until the tears stopped. "Come," he said. "I will hold thee." The deliberate use of the word *thee* had a salutary effect on the child.

"Thee must take *me* now," Cub said.

The track took a slow turning and then they were in the meadow ringed with beech trees. Not a blade of grass stirred between the bodies. The busy, scurrying ants were gone.

The oddest thing, he thought, *is that there is not much blood. Not a flood of it. Not a meadowful.* Just bodies strewn about as though they were dollies flung down by a careless child.

They found the dark-haired scar-faced woman first, lying on her back, her arms spread wide as if welcoming her death. Near her were two of the boys, side by side. Close by them, a third boy and one of the wild men.

He held the child against his shoulder. "Do not look," he cautioned, though he knew from the rigid body that the child was taking it all in. "Do not look."

He wandered across the field of death until he heard an awful sound. It was a dog howling, the cry long and low. He wondered that he had not heard it before. Following the thread of it, he came to the meadow's edge and there was the wodewose and, with him, Fowler. They were locked in an awful embrace. It was Fowler's dog, Ranger, who was howling, his muzzle muddied with blood. When he saw the boys, he shut up and lay down miserably, head on paws, following their every movement with liquid eyes.

"Stay, Ranger," Hawk-Hobby said, trying to put iron in his command.

The dog did not move toward them and, after a minute, Hawk-Hobby put the child down, and examined the dead men.

It was clear to see how it had happened. The wodewose's hands were tightly wrapped around

Fowler's neck, so tightly the traitor's eyes bulged and his tongue protruded from his mouth. Out of the wild man's back stuck the haft of a soldier's spear, and around that wound were bite marks. Which of the two of them had died first hardly mattered.

"Make him live, Dreamer," the child whispered. "Make him live."

Hawk-Hobby took the wodewose by the shoulder and brought the ruined head close to his own. The wild man was stiff with death, his lips parted in a final agony. It was all the boy could do to touch him.

"Give him breath, Dreamer," the child whispered again.

Bending over, though he shook with the horror of it, Hawk-Hobby blew the breath of life into the grimace of a mouth.

Once, twice, three times he blew. Then waited. Then blew again.

He closed his eyes and remembered his dream of breath, remembered how it had felt when he had given life to the little bird. He prayed, sudden tears running down his cheeks.

He blew again.

And again.

And nothing happened.

Nothing at all.

"Make him live, Dreamer," the child begged.

Let him live, the boy prayed.

But his magic—capricious, wanton, unpredictable—did not come at his calling.

15. FAMILY

HOW LONG THEY SAT THERE BY THE DEAD men, Hawk-Hobby did not know. But eventually the dog came over to him and licked his hand several times as if learning the taste.

The boy stood. "Come," he said. "It is time for us to go." And the three of them—boy, child, dog—walked together to the edge of the meadow, leaving the dead behind.

"Why did he not live?" Cub asked.

Hawk-Hobby shook his head. "I do not know," he said. "I do not know near enough yet. But I will learn." He looked into the child's face, now streaked with dirt and tears. "I promise you I will learn."

"I will learn, too," the child said to him confidently. "And 'ee will teach me."

They went down the path, but in the opposite direction than the soldiers had taken. The dog ranged ahead, then returned, over and over and over again, as if to satisfy himself the two were safe.

They did not stop until the sun was well overhead.

In a little glade, where berries grew in profusion, they had a meal. In between one juicy handful and the next, Cub turned to the boy. "Are thee my father now?" he asked.

Startled, Hawk-Hobby smiled slowly. The idea was new to him. All this while he had been seeking a father for himself. Now, it seemed, he had a son. "If you wish it."

In answer, the child put his hand in the boy's.

"Then perhaps," Hawk-Hobby said, "if we are to be a family, we need to tell one another our true names."

"But—'ee are Dreamer," the child said. "Robin o' the Wood."

"No," the boy answered, kneeling before the child. "I am a dreamer, true, but that is not my true name. My name..." He took a deep breath. "My name is Merlin."

"Like the hawk?" the child asked. "I like hawks."

"Like the hawk. And someday I shall teach you how to tame them as I was taught," Merlin said. "But now I have many other things to teach you. Such as what your place is in this world. And that you must not rise to the lure. And..."

"But *my* name, Merlin. What be 'ee calling me?"

"Cub."

"Can I be bigger than a cub?"

"You will be in time."

"As big as...as big as a bear? Then no one could kill what is mine. If I be big and powerful as a bear."

Merlin smiled. "As big as a bear, certainly," he said. "But if you are a bear, Cub, then we shall call you Artus, for that means bear-man." As he said it, he suddenly remembered his dream of the bear. Perhaps, perhaps this was meant, after all.

"Artus. Artus. Artus," the child cried out, twirling around and around until he was quite dizzy with it.

At the sound of the child's name, the dog burst out of the woods and ran about the two of them, barking.

"Ranger," commanded Merlin, "do your duty to this King Bear."

Inexplicably, the dog stopped and bowed its head. Then, when Artus laughed delightedly, and clapped his berry-stained hands, the dog turned and ran back down the path as if to scout the long, perilous way.

Light.

Morn.

"How can I continue, how can I rule now that he is gone?"

"You are king, my lord. He was just an old mage. And he lacked all humility."

"Hush. He was my father. He was my teacher. He was my friend."

"A king has no friends, my lord."

"Not even you, Gwen?"

"Not even me, Arthur."

"You are wrong, you know. He was my friend from the first moment I saw him. Though I did not

know then—or ever—what he truly was. Sometimes he seemed to me to be as fierce as a wild dog, sometimes as busy as an ant, ofttimes as slippery as a trout. He was a hawk, a hobby, a merlin."

"He was a man, my lord."

"Not a man like me, Gwen."

"No one is like you, Arthur."

"No one?"

"You are the king."

"So am I powerful?"

"Very powerful."

"That is good. If I am powerful, then no one can hurt me. Or mine. So why do I hurt so now that he is gone?"

And he calls his servants to him with a bell that sounds like a tamed hawk's jesses, like the sound of spears clashing on earth, that place perilously juxtaposed between heaven and hell.

AUTHOR'S NOTE

The story of Merlin, King Arthur's great court wizard, is not one story but many, told by different tellers over nearly fifteen centuries. In some of the tales he is a Druid priest. In others, a seer. In still others he is a shape-shifter, a dream-reader, a wild man in the woods.

And in some of the old tales, Merlin is a child born of a princess in a nunnery, his father a demon.

In the Middle Ages, because of wars or famine or plague, many children were actually abandoned in the woods. There they were left to—in the Latin ecclesiastical phrase—*aliena misericordia*—the kindness of strangers. Historically, until the eighteenth century, the rate of known abandonments in some parts of Europe was as high as one in four children, an astonishing and appalling figure.

Hawking, or falconry, is the art of using falcons, hawks—even eagles and owls—in hunting game. It is a very ancient pastime, practiced by humans even before they learned to write. Falconers have their own special words: a male hawk (which is smaller than the female) is called a *tercel*. The larger female hawk is called a *falcon*. An *eyas* is a hawk taken from the nest when fully fledged but as yet unable to fly. But the wild-caught immature bird is a *passager*.

A *merlin* is a small falcon, sometimes called a pigeon hawk in America. It was once much used in English falconry.

The only story told of Merlin's childhood handed down from the Middle Ages is that he is a fatherless Welsh princeling who has prophetic dreams about red and white dragons. In the story he tells this dream—under threat of execution—to the usurping King Vortigern. He explains that the dream is about Vortigern's battle tower, which has been collapsing. Under the boy's instructions, the tower is made to

DATE DUE